GALOS; Z J

FIGHTING STANCE

Novel

Impressum

Bibliographical Information of the German National Library.
The German National Library indexes this publication with the German National Bibliography.
Detailed bibliographical data may be derived from the Internet website http://dnb.dnb.de

©2020 GALOS; Z J
Producer and publisher: BoD-Books on Demand, Norderstedt.

ISBN: 9783751902304

PROLOG

He was the golden boy of his village. They called him chryso agori, or short chryso. With his athletic figure, his sporting activities came naturally to him. He competed with an inert fun of living a life in a relative unbridled freedom, and he was always way ahead of his classes and colleagues, winning most competitions. His parents were pleased with his growing up and considering his talents, they arranged for his private tuition in studying anatomy and the basic training in the Olympic disciplines.

Watching movies, he took a liking to Chinese and Japanese movies with their dream-like demonstrations of smooth body movements flying around on roofs and in space while fighting. The modern Kung-Fu-style of movies enticed his fantasy. Daily walks to the beach on the island of Delos, inspired him not only mentally, but he started to imitate the flowing dancing styles of Ti Chi fighters. The physical and mentally balance, he felt after his exercises, gave him a glow of harmony that reflected on his appearance. People bowed to him, as if he would emerge as a demi-god born from the crest of the Mediterranean Sea.

As he grew up into a handsome men with gilded curly hair, many young women adored him, especially watching sporting events and competitions. Soon he had a fan club, his parents administered for him. Taking up an interest in traveling, he arrived in the USA, where he met a friend who introduced him to Tai Chi martial arts. He was soon hooked on this sport and he mastered his classes with distinction. His career as a Tai Chi sports-educator seemed to be the choice for him, as he won his first European championship in the martial art section.

But his love for Greece let him return time and again, to see his parents, who helped him to establish his own Tai Chi Club, from his earnings. It became a well-known venue for sporting events, with an emphasis for Tai Chi martial art. His intentions were to stage a European championship event, besides to extend this local venue to become a place of sports and worship. Tai Chi sport had led him to the philosophy of LaoTse and the studies of Taoism based on the history of Tai Chi and its growing popularity. Were martial arts a way of practicing Taoism? Certainly Tai Chi served also for health benefits, and it also became popular for self-defense worldwide, even if the Western society had originally a cautionary approach to this culture.

Chapter One.
Goran.

His movements are swift and elegant. The aesthetics of Tai Chi are all important to him, especially stances. One recalls animals and at times a butterfly, being here and there, resting for a few seconds with sudden bursts of movements that are of dire consequence to his opponent, and certainly deadly to his enemies in battle. Yet he always seems a dancer, fleet-footed with bursts of speed and in repose as if frozen for a moment, to gain the concentration resorting back to his inner and outer balance he'll need to finally overthrow his opponent with harmonious arm movements. And at times it looks a confusing exchange of fast and furious arm movements, pushing hands, as it's called in general terms, trying to catch the opponent for a throw. It becomes faster, more furious and reminds Kathy of *kungfu* movies she had watched with Goran, when he studied other fighters in various disciplines.

Goran seems to have slowed down and his opponent senses an opportunity for a throw, but just as he attacks and thinks he has gained control of a move, Goran turns with the speed of a feral cat and catching his opponent unaware throws him to the floor. There's big applause from the Goran camp, who wants their favourite fighter to win. At the opposite side the hall the supporters of his opponent are quiet, some are booing, with a dusky man in their midst looking angry.

"It is wonderful to watch Goran, don't you think?' Kathy addresses her friend Susan; she had asked to accompany her to the quarterfinals of the local championship, where Goran is contender for the top spot again.

"I do not understand much of martial arts," Susan replies, "but it certainly draws one into its ban." Kathy smiles. "I guess I am biased,"

"After all he is an exceptional man, Kathy."

"I adore him, venerate him and I am in love with him."

"I am glad for you Kathy."

The fight has passed its main part and Goran leads the scoreboard. The gong announces the end of the fight. Goran is declared the winner by points. Kathy jumps up with joy and sends a kiss to Goran who bows.

While the two friends have a drink at the adjoining cafe waiting for Goran to fetch them, Kathy congratulates him on her cellphone. Shortly thereafter Goran calls her back.

"He'll be here in 10 minutes," Kathy tells Susan, whose emergency beeper signals and she checks it.

"Unfortunately, I have to go now Kathy, a patient needs my urgent attention.

"Pity you cannot meet Goran, but I appreciate you could come at such short notice."

"Sometimes I have a chance to sneak out." She smiles. "Bye Kathy, stay in touch."

"Bye Susan, seeing you sometime soon."

"All right, when I have another chance to get away." Kathy watches her friend move and she muses about her. What a wonderful person Susan is, always ready to help people in need, especially in the burns unit, she had put up from her fundraising: Selfless and capable, one of the best maxillofacial surgeons in Europe. It had been not an easy start for Susan. She had been sponsored by a wealthy eccentric, marked by a bouts of sexual deviation, during which he abused her. However she wanted to be a surgeon and financed her studies by succumbing to her sponsor's unusual needs.

"A penny for your thoughts."

"Hi Goran," Kathy kissed him. "Congratulations for your win."

"Thanks, it was not an easy fight."

"But you did well Goran." He smiles at her with a boyish grin, his lips curling. Kathy loves this expression, the one she remembers best when she fell in love with him the first time.

"Where is your friend?" Kathy stirs.

"Oh you mean Susan. She had to run off to a patient."

"Ah doctors are always on the move."

"She promised to keep in touch. Perhaps we can arrange a lunch?"

"Certainly. I would like to meet her."

"Let's go Goran; I have booked a table at your favourite restaurant."

"In that case I am ready."

"All right. I drive." Kathy takes his arm and Goran's sinewy body touches hers for a moment. A spark of electricity enters Kathy's thighs and she is stirred. Wow, she thinks, one touch and she is feeling all ready for his embrace. It is wonderful to love Goran and sense that our libidos are working so strong. She presses the remote to her car and Goran opens the door for her. She swings into her seat with her mini dress sliding up her legs. Goran joins her and he gazes at Kathy's legs. She has started the car and drives off. Goran places his hand on her thigh. Kathy looks at him shortly and a pleasurable feeling chases up her spine. Kathy drives the short distance from the club to the restaurant. Goran's hand aroused her and she opens her legs slightly. By the time they arrive at the restaurant she senses that Goran is ready for some more intimacy. She parks the car. Then she cannot wait to embrace him. They kiss and she touches him. He is aroused.

"I want you Goran."

"I want you too Kathy."

"It's not possible to do it in the car." Kathy fantasizes about it.

"Let's try the backseat." Goran smiles and opens the back door, takes a seat and waits for Cathy to follow. Kathy's sexual appetite heightened, she falls over Goran's body, opens his waist button and lowering his pants she starts devouring him. Their body heat is misting up the windows. Goran slides his hand below her soft top. Their intimacy is intense and Goran peaks.

"Kathy you were wonderful, how I enjoy your oral attention."

"I love all of you Goran, my man!" Kathy cleans Goran up and they adjust their clothes. Kathy locks her Subaru and both head toward the restaurant's facilities to clean up.

The maître welcomes them.

"Ah, Mr Goran, nice to see you again and beautiful Mrs Cathy."

"Good day Alexandros, nice being here." The maître takes them to Goran's usual table overlooking the Saronic Gulf. Goran gazes at Kathy, still in awe of her seducing skills. 'The kiss of life' she calls it. Goran smiles.

"Look Goran how wonderful calm the sea looks today."

"It is you who look wonderful," he says and Kathy takes his hands and squeezes them. Their knees meet below the table. Goran feels a new sensation through Kathy's touches and as he gazes into her eyes, he feels great desire for her moving his hand below the tablecloth and touching Kathy's inner thighs. "Oh Goran," she moans, "You have the sparks to arouse me again." He looks into her eyes that have taken on the blue-green colour of the sea. A scent of jasmine is in the air from a bowl of flowers nearby. She is so special to me, Goran muses. My hurting from the fight is gone and I feel like a reborn child. Kathy looks into Goran's eyes that have a lively brown sprinkling around his iris that had become translucent green.

"We complement each other Goran," she coos, but by now my stomach grumbles."

"OK, let's order Kathy." He winks at the maitre'd who takes their orders.

Chapter Two
Caltis & Takis

Caltis wakes from interrupted sleep. He feels mentally drained but his body is tensed up and he has to get rid of pent-up energies mixed with his desperation of finding money to pay Nanos the interest on his loan. It is a never-ending task of avoiding executing myself, he thinks aloud, murmuring as he sits up in bed. In his dreams he saw himself standing on a box with a noose around his neck. Nasos the loan shark sits in a chair opposite, his foot leaning against a box.
"You have not paid me the interest this month." His foot pushes against the box. Caltis feels the nooses tightening around his neck.
"I will get it tomorrow."
"You said that last week." Nasos grins and lights up a cigar. The acrid smell wafts toward Caltis and he has to cough.
"Stop torturing me Nasos."
"I will if you pay me my interest due."
"I have some money."
"Oh, you have?" Nasos foot pushes against the box again and Celtis fears to tumble down and strangle himself.
"If you take me down I will give it to you."

"Hah, no way, tell me where it is and I will consider if it's enough. Celtis directs Nasos to his metal chest. Nasos looks for the cash.

"It's only 300 and the interest is 500 this month."

"It's all I have left for food."

"Sorry chum, but that's not good. You have to go I am afraid." Nasos kicks the box and …Caltis wakes. Sweat covers his forehead. "Damned dream," he mumbles, "I must have dozed off again."

I have to win the European Masters championships, even if I have to get Goran out of the way. Dark thoughts infuse his mind and he thinks about ways to get rid of Goran. He showers and when he towels himself off. His strategy to reach his goal and rid himself of debt shapes in his mind: First, he has to assemble his gang, as he has to stay officially clean and only pull the threads. He cannot risk that somebody would detect him being involved with neutralizing Goran. Everybody in the club knows that he is on a highly competitive footing with Goran that borders on a hateful relationship and the club members are already divided about it. Goran still holds a majority share in the Martial Arts clubs and most members stand by the 'Chrysos Iroas' - The Golden Hero - as he is called by all his fans, especially as he is popular with all women. Caltis feels a twang of deep-rooted jealousy pervading his innermost core and he bangs his fist on the breakfast table. A glass of tomato juice tumbles and crashes onto the tiled floor, a puddle forms on the white tiles and it looks like blood. "Death to Goran," he shouts. A startled neighbour's shepherd dog close to the window starts barking.

He rushes to his desk and writes the names of his former army buddies into his diary. Then he picks the names from his address book and adds the phone numbers. He dials the first one, Takis. He is not available, so he leaves a message. He continues through his list of ten names. At the fourth name, Georgios, he leaves a message on his answering machine. By the time he dials the eighth name, he gets a direct connection. "Altis," he recalls the voice of his former army buddy. "It's Caltis." There's a short pause on the other end. "Geewas Caltis, for a moment I was not sure if it is you."

"How are you Altis?"

"Thank you, not too bad."

"You sound as if you have trouble." Altis coughs.

"Well, who has no trouble nowadays?"

"Indeed, tell me."

"What can I do for you, Caltis?"

"Well it's not a matter I wish to discuss on the telephone, could we meet?" Altis pauses and rasps.

"Yes, if that's the case, I have my day off tomorrow"

"OK, let's meet at the old windmill outside town. I let you know the time."

While Caltis prepares his notes and tools, his mobile phone rings. It's Takis.

"Hi Takis, could you come to the old windmill in an hour's time?"

"Is it urgent?"

"Yes,"

"OK, I will be there." Caltis takes his notes and his knapsack with him, where he keeps basic tools, just in case he has to force a lock.

Caltis muses about the prompt reply from Takis. It seems that he was prepared to meet him. Well I have emphasized that it's urgent, Caltis thinks, but I never thought he would be ready at short notice. Yet I had saved his life once in a brawl, perhaps he feels that he owes me.

Caltis leaves a note for his daughter to phone her Mom and see how she is doing and that he had urgent business and will be home later as usual. Then he steps into his Fiat 600 and drives the short distance from his apartment toward Voulagmeni motorway heading out of town.

Takis arrives minutes after Caltis, who had already opened the door with his set of burglar-tools, he still kept from his time when he worked as a locksmith. It comes handy now; he murmurs, places the lock picking tools back into his knapsack, fixes a new lock onto the wooden oak door and tests its operation. Perfect.

"Hi Caltis!" Takis emerges from his blue Hyundai, he keeps washed and waxed.

"Hi Takis." Caltis embraces his old army friend. "Long time no see."

"Indeed, but I have a good idea that it will change from now on," Caltis replies. "Let's go inside, I have changed the lock." Caltis notices that Takis has kept in good shape.

"I recall your lock-picking skills from back in army times." Caltis laughs.

"Let's check the place out." It is poorly lit from small and dirty windows. He climbs the wooden stair that squeaks now and then, but all seems in good working order. On the first floor they find a table and some chairs. Caltis takes a rag and wipes the table and then a chair.

"Not even much dust, the window frames seem to be in good condition.

"They do not build like this anymore." Takis replies and pulls up a chair dusting off its wooden seat, when joins Caltis who had seated himself and taken his notebook from his knapsack.

"Now Takis, I have found your details on the Internet and thought about to call you first, as we go back a long way and have been best of army buddies."

"Yes, true, I am glad you phoned me Caltis." He rolls his eyes as if he would thank a deity up in heaven.

"Are you in trouble?"

"Well I have lost my job as an accountant in a multinational firm."

"Well, of course you could carry on to take that job with the company I intend to form," Caltis replies. Takis' eyes light up and he sighs.

"That would be just great! Tell me about it." Caltis moves his seating position getting closer to Takis as if he would confide him.

"It's top secret Takis, and I am relying on your absolute discretion trusting you with what I have to say like a partner in crime."

"Yes, like old times at the army. Not a word about our secrets ever came out of my mouth!"

"Yes, that's it. Now let me tell you." A sudden sound startles them. It came from upstairs.

"Damned, somebody here?" Caltis shouts. "Let's check it out!" He takes a torch from his knapsack. The wooden stairs to the second floor were of smaller width and there was only a handrail at the rough plastered wall. As Caltis arrives on the tiny top floor, something grazes his hair. He steps back and directs the beam of his torch upwards. Skeletal feet dangle in front of him. He searches higher. In his beam of light the dried out skeleton of a woman becomes visible, hanging from a rope tied around her neck. Her skin dried out like a mummy's. "Look at this!" Turning to Takis, he points at the horrid scene in the semi-darkness. Takis says nothing. "She must have been murdered, Caltis says, "look at her belly."

"Indeed it still shows a bulge, as if she was pregnant, but she has dried out up here completely."

"I guess whoever did this had knowledge about mummification. The corpse is over 10 years here and her features are clear and recognizable."

"You could be right "Takis replies, "we have to get outta here!"

"Don't panic Takis; this has nothing to do with us. Besides it will be a symbol for our secrecy." Caltis grinned as he looked at Takis' frightened face.

"How do you mean?"

"I will tell you soon. Let's go back to the bigger floor below."

"We have to open a window."

"No! The smell would give it away." At that moment a crow flies down toward Takis' head. Caltis took a piece of wood nearby and shouted at Takis to duck. With one well-aimed hit he killed the black bird, hitting it again on the floor. "It must have feasted on the corpse."

"It's a bad omen," whispered Takis, "but how did the bird ever get in here?"

Caltis pointed to a small hole around a rafter of the roof support. "There. It must have entered as a small bird sensing the corpse."

"Let's have a drink." Caltis took a bottle of tsipouro from his knapsack and filled two plastic beakers. "Cheers!"

"Yamas," Takis replies, as he prefers toasting .in Greek. Caltis refills the cups. After some drinks the gruesome find of the skeleton has lost its initial hair-raising impact on the friends and Caltis explains to Takis between cups of the clear white and potent drink his intention to form a brotherhood, a gang that will go through thick and thin. "Like brothers," he utters as the alcohol seeps into his blood and affects his speech.

"Like Spartan brothers," Takis lulls and downs another cup.

"I am glad you are with me, Takis," Caltis joins his toast. With the bottle half empty, Takis uses the torch, setting it on the table and he takes a candle from his knapsack lighting it. Stay here Takis, while I check out if this candlelight is visible through the higher windows to the outside." He walks down the stairs and switching the torch off, opens the door and walks around the windmill in spiraling greater circles until he has convinced himself that there is nothing to be seen, with the few windows all remaining dark. However, he will place black curtains onto the windows as the beam of the torch walking up the stairs, where most windows are placed, could give away their presence. He will ask Takis to arrange the blackout curtains, as he knows somebody at an alteration shop. When Caltis arrives back he notices Takis snoozing, with his head on the table.

"Takis, Takis, wake up!" Takis stirs.

"Must have dozed off," Takis mumbles.

"We need some coffee," Caltis says.

"Let's drive to the next espresso bar." Takis agrees.

Chapter Three
Kathy & Susan

Kathy meets Susan in the hall of the Martial Arts Club where Goran will be fighting in the finals for the local championships. There is a buzz of a crowd filling the hall to capacity. Susan tried to be in time, but an urgent matter had held her back at her clinic, yet she could leave to reach the championships at half time, when Goran's fight would start.

"Hi Susan, glad you could make it."

"Thanks Kathy for the invite, unfortunately I could not attend the social gathering ahead of the fight."

"It's all right Susan; I will introduce Goran to you another time." The bell sounds for the finals to start in a few minutes. Kathy has reserved a seat for Susan. The seats are excellent overlooking the area of a blue mat, indicating the fighting area. Kathy is nervous and she cannot hide her emotion. Susan sensing it takes Kathy's hand. A relief from tension flows from Kathy to Susan, who experiences a tickling of her erotic spots, as if she would have been touched on her nipples. Kathy had watched Susan's reaction as parts of her nervousness abides. She observes Susan's nipples growing hard through the soft cotton of her top. She smiles, Susan has a great liking of her and it is erotic. She had no idea why Susan had attracted her when she met her at first at the clinic for facial reconstruction, where she had accompanied a friend, who had a bike accident and his torn off ear had to be attended to. As she visited, she involved Susan in discussions about her work as a surgeon. Besides having gained great respect for her skills and surgical successes, Susan could not find time enough to follow Kathy's invitations, until now. The good chemistry between them had taken off to a friendship that became closer with each meeting. Kathy knew that Susan would become more than a friend, perhaps a soulmate, a love interest or a curious partner for an experiment with gender love. She was attractive and sensual, intelligent and highly skilled in her profession. Kathy, the artist sensed her need for intimacy with women. She sketched images of Susan into her journal and added lines of poetry about her.

"Thanks Susan," Kathy smiled at her.

"My pleasure, I hope I have taken away some of your nervousness."

"Indeed, I am tense. This fight means so much for Goran."

"You have deep feelings for him."

"Yes, but today…"she bent over to whisper into Susan's ear," I have suddenly felt great feelings for you." Susan's heart missed a beat and then she felt her heart beating faster, as if some electric current had been connected to her.

"I am so glad Kathy," she said, a warm glance flashed in her eyes. The gong sounded and the fight began. Kathy withdrew her fingers from Susan's warm hand. She balled fists to help Goran make his moves and swing his arms, but Goran seemed somewhat slower as usual. She felt a rush of cold along her spine, as the two Tai Chi fighters started to warm-up and pushing hands slower for starters, until Goran landed on the mat, but recovered quickly with a side roll pushing himself quickly to his feet. Susan was afraid for Goran to fall behind his opponent in points, but Goran had the more appealing aesthetics of his movements that gave him equal points. Kathy missed the warmth of Susan's hand and she clapped her hands when Goran made a point and slowly warmed up for his famous stances which changed from horse stance to bow stance with flat and resting stances alternating. He tried to find the weaknesses of his fighting partner, who was equal in skills to him. Goran went quickly through the register of attack modes to see where he could score against his hard hitting opponent. He began a furious onslaught of pushing hands and their combat sounded like a flurry of bird's wings in flight. Kathy moved her legs, her knee touching Susan's, who seemed to enjoy their body contact, as she did not mover her foot away. Every time Goran would throw his opponent, she would grab Susan's hand and squeeze it. It gave her a rising feeling as if she would be having a foreplay with Goran. In a way it became that as Goran had to train hard for weeks on end and they had no time for a night together. So all her sexual energy streamed into Susan, who became increasingly charged with Kathy's eroticism until she felt she would explode. But Kathy sensed Susan's desires for intimacy with her and she withdrew the moment she sensed her arousal. This game lasted and Susan desired more. Her eyes were on the fight, but her heart sneaked closer to Kathy's heart, whose body talk gave her away: I- want-you-Susan. Susan's inner voice responded -Yes, love, yes! It started to make her cheeks hot. She was afraid to blush.

The movements of the fighters became more entangled in greater speed and their footwork became like a dance with continual changes of stance. Just as Goran had changed his foot technique, pulling his opponent wide and throw him to the mat, he came back in a jiffy for another round of spectacular hand pushing. The points were very close, changing sides regularly meant that the fighters were equal and extra time had to be allowed to decide the winner.

At one stage when Goran was behind on points, he looked into Kathy's direction for inspiration and Kathy send him a kiss. This seemed to raise his strength and while he remained in a resting stance he concentrated, then suddenly he attacked. Not with force but technique and jumps, this surprised his opponent, a less enthusiastic jumper, but more a hard hitter. Goran had finally found the weakness of his opponent, using his fierce strength to soft land his punches and use the momentum to throw him to the mat. Kathy was jumping up embracing Susan. When their bodies touched, a spark connected the friends instantly stirring them up on a spiral.

"Goran is leading, Goran is leading," she shouted to the handclapping of the crowd. "I love you Susan, soulmate," she whispered into Susan's ear. Finally after more time Goran seemed on a winning streak and his fine art of Tai Chi celebration with body aesthetics lifted him above his opponent, who faded, sapped of strength. Goran had used his opponent's strength to become the victor. Kathy pulled the hand of Susan to follow her out of the hall before the masses would block the exits. Straight to the ladies rooms, she closed the door and hugged Susan kissing her. The rush of Kathy's adrenalin had inflamed Susan and she kissed Kathy back with passion.

"Come into the cubicle," Kathy pulled Susan behind her. She locked the door and her hands caressed Susan's breast. At the same time Susan's hands caressed Kathy's hair, whose head slid down to her belly. A feverish shower raced through Susan, as she wished Kathy to eat her up right now. Kathy touched Susan's pussy through her pants. She sat down on the low wall mounted toilet bowl and Susan spread her legs standing in front of her. Kathy opened Susan's waits button and her pants slid down her thighs. She wore thongs and her pussy was warm and moist as Kathy slid her finger along her vulva. The moment Kathy's lips met Susan's pussy a moan escaped from Susa's lips.

"I love eating you up," Kathy whispered as she took a breather. Susan pushed herself toward Kathy and arched back as she felt a warm sensation that spiraled her up into the air. She sensed that she was close to her height as Kathy's experienced cunnilingus brought her to a soft cry. The sensation of a height had been close to a great orgasm, she remembered she had a long time ago. She lifted Kathy up and kissed her with passion, pushing her top up and kissing her breasts, rubbing her nipples and bringing Kathy to an instant height. Then she rested, suddenly drained from energy, but she recovered as soon as Kathy kissed her, replenishing her lost energies. "We have to clean up," Kathy said. "Pity, you taste so good and smell so good"

"But I want you" Susan whispered.

"There will be time for that later," Kathy said, "Right now I have to go to see Goran in his restroom." Susan's emergency phone beeped. "I have to go," she said, "emergency."

"Keep in touch Kathy."

"I will and I am looking forward to our next meeting."

"Indeed, so do I. It will be my turn next time!"

"I am wet already," Kathy teased Susan and embraced her. Kathy cleaned up applied her favourite Dior perfume Goran liked so much and rushed through the passage to the restroom area, showing her access card to security.

"Kathy," exclaimed Goran as she entered his room. He lay with a sheet covered on the massage table, having finished a while ago.

"Congratulations Goran, Kathy came closer and kissed him. He pulled her down and kissed her with passion, surprising her. He still has such strength, Kathy thought. I feel stirred. "Lock the door Kathy," Goran whispered to her.

"What have we here? Kathy's fingers moved the linen cover and her head moved down Goran's body. He moaned and whispered endearments to her, while she began her erotic ritual, adoring his erection. Kathy had great skills in oral sex and while she teased his hard-on, pictures of Susan appeared in her mind's eye. The flashbacks seemed as if Goran would be intimate with them both in a threesome. As soon as she had rid herself of her garb, she straddled him and rode him like an Amazon. Goran endured but the fight had made him weak and he could only climax after Kathy's skillful joyride, turning midway around on him showing him her perfectly shaped back.

"I love you Kathy." Goran whispered and dozed off into a healing slumber. Kathy cleaned herself and dressed. Then she opened the fridge, took out a prepared beef soup package and placed it into a casserole, which she put onto a warming plate. Goran disliked microwave cooked food. When he had rested enough, some hot nutritious food would be awaiting him.

Chapter Four
Nasos

Nanos rises early after a good night's sleep. He drops his pajamas in his bathroom clad in black stone, with indirect lighting and a full-height mirror stretches his appearance. He likes to live in his morning's world illusion that he is indeed a handsome prince of the mysterious lands across the Aegean Seas, living as a recluse artist on a godforsaken part of an island, he calls 'Nanoland'. He is pleased with his narcissistic admiration of his body, especially with his well-endowed penis, which seems to contradict his real body, but here in the distortion of a curved mirror, especially made for him, his body is in perfect proportion to his huge phallus, his most precious body part he celebrates with his many virtual girlfriends on the Internet, switching on his webcam, when he takes a bath in his Jacuzzi tub. He had offers from porn movie producers, but he agreed to adequate payment for using footage from his 'Nanoland' bathroom, where lighting and his image in his curved mirror made a perfect background for a movie clip. Nanos is fanatical about his privacy, where he remains king of nudes, as customers who have heard of his pedophile activities, call him Priapus, symbol of Pan's sexual prowess. Nanos is a hybrid of nature, a hermaphrodite in his complex psyche, an individual whose mind is as distorted as his encumbered body features in the mirror image of himself. Nanos' dwarf-like appearance with a hunchback on top of his repulsive appearance sees himself as an attractive man, who is adored by boys who are in awe of his huge penis and gay men are drawn to him for the physical pleasure he gives them against payment. Few women are attracted to him, but once the word about his huge penis has made the rounds in the posh suburb of the city, curiosity takes them to appear in pairs, become friends and celebrate his sexual prowess.

He has an aversion against taking his precious Jaguar to his downtown office, which is situated on the first floor in a building adjacent to the four stars Acropolis hotel. Nanos is well known in the underworld and assured of continuous protection, as he pays well and he has to afford it, as too many enemies lurk in the dark to get a hit on the ugly loan shark. He has carefully dressed in his tailored suit, wearing a bullet-proof vest and he exits his home, activates the alarm and walks to his car. He constantly wonders if his security guards are trained sufficiently to protect him, but he has been assured by his underground partners-in-crime that all entrances and exits to his lair are covered, besides, as they have a share in his lucrative business they better look after their investment. Nanos exits the garage, locks his car by remote and enters the specific lift that has a security card access and stops only at his floor and two floors higher up where security keeps an office and a temporary safe place for their members, who fell out with the law. Nanos dislikes sharing a lift with others, as he constantly fears for his life, having a fanatical drive to be in absolute control of his life.

He opens the door to his offices with his access card, which lets him enter into a lobby, where he opens the control box with another swipe of his card and disarms the alarm system, switching it to intruder stand-by. Anyone entering the lobby illegally will be caught on camera and the alarm system would lock all doors instantly. Then security would analyze the pictures and deal with the culprit. Through years Nanos has been trained properly in tactics of dealing with people loaning money from him and all aspects of squeezing them for galloping interests rates until they are broke having paid the loan back many times and had to be disposed of. He thought of it as business and being disfigured from an early age, he has been hardened against the kicks of his classmates and arrogant gang members, until John the Caesar, had picked him up and secured him a place in his growing illegal organization. As Nanos had a knack for figures, he was an ideal partner looking after the Caesar's twin books: The red book for his private fortune and the black book for his official business with the underworld. Nasos proved to be an excellent accountant and having no assistants made him even more powerful in time. He would never afford others to enter his solitary life and nobody knew his patterns of movement. He demanded a day of warning with appointments and a confirmation of arrival half an hour before.

He checked his gun safe and deactivated the electronic lock. The weapons were neat, cleaned and ready for action if necessary. Besides he kept a loaded magnum six shooter in the drawer of his office desk. He hated to be surprised. Loving movies he watched from an Internet source, his mind spun out possibilities to overcome his alarm system and that he wanted to face with powerful weaponry, be ready and alert at all times. John, his mentor had promoted him to his right hand man and he taught him martial arts and urged him to visit him at his property for regular shooting practice and bouts of martial art games, in which John had skills and experience.

Nasos retrieved his leather bound diary from his locked drawers and reviewed his activities mapped out for the day. This diary contained names of people who had borrowed money from him. Besides laundering the cash that way, he received an enormeous amount of clean interest money as return, he and John used to share for their expenses and for investments where money was electronically checked. Besides Nasos had a checking device himself and he reassured himself of the cash payments that they were clean and free of counterfeits.

This reminded him of checking the upcoming payments from his customers. Ah, there was this man Caltis, martial art specialist and contender for the European Masters Championships. Nasos did not like him but John had agreed to loan him money, as he appeared to be a martial arts fighter, John considered as brothers. However, Nasos told John that he will have to squeeze him for interest real hard, as he appeared to be living a relatively good life and he spent money on women. Just charge him normal rates, John told Nasos, who had other thoughts about this man. He had seen him with his young daughter, a child-woman, Nasos had been attracted to. He smacked his lips as he thought of her mini skirt and her shapely legs. When Caltis had approached Nasos, he came along with her having fetched her from school. She had only her training gear on without underwear and Nasos feasted his eyes on her shapely figure in her tight outfit, while she had set her eyes on his bulging crotch.

As Caltis was a recommendation by John, his senior partner, Nasos has been lenient to hunt him down for a day or two past his due date for interest money. But this time he was overdue already for a week. He had to summon him to his office, as it was safer to meet here than at the Club where Caltis trained every day for his forthcoming fights.

Caltis received Nasos' phone call when he relaxed in the hot tub at the club. He immediately froze as Nasos called for the pending interest payment on his substantial loan. Meeting at Nanos' secured fortress, Caltis seemed monosyllabic as if he was holding back.

"You know what happens to people who do not pay on time?" Nasos started his routine of intimidating the dark skinned man who rose from a street fighter to a martial arts expert in short time, but had lived beyond his means. "You have to have the interest payment delivered here in person by noon tomorrow, or there will be dire consequences." Nasos spoke with a soft voice, a trademark of powerful men. Caltis froze, his body started to shiver.

"I will try hard but I am waiting for a payment myself."

"Then speed it up, tomorrow noon at my office." Nasos cut the connection. He sensed trouble with this man, as he already had a bad gutfeel right from the start when he met him. Whatever John thought of this man of being a brother, he had messed up on keeping to his agreement and contract. Nasos suspected that Caltis would default and he thought about his next move. Well, he has a pretty daughter, he smacked his lips. If John would think that he would be soft on his brother in arms, he had to be disappointed. A contract is a contract. Fuck John, he would raise the interest to double, that'll teach him for next time. However he would only pay the interest if he would otherwise lose his daughter. Nasos grinned.

Chapter Five
Elena

The Martial Arts Club, located on the southern stretch of an Athenian suburb, along its famous string of beaches, also known as the local Riviera, is a low rise building with the main entrance hall adjacent to the private and public parking area. The hallway with its marble paving leads with a descending passage to sets of public toilets. Further passages give access to the main competition sports hall on a terraced design position toward the sea. The visitors are guided to their elevated seats arranged around the rectangular layout, with the judges seated alongside the coloured mat area that demarcates the competition zone for the fighters. It has been named 'The Box' as due to its dominant shape, geometrical and minimalist in its design approach, it had been constructed to a tight budget. Behind the main hall there are two practice areas that are located on a lower level, close to the change rooms and their toilets, the washrooms for the club members and the participants in the sport of martial art.

From the public areas an extension of a passage leads to the café and a restaurant section, where club members use the space to celebrate events. The dining hall's main feature, an entirely full-height glazed wall, opens up to the Saronic Gulf, with a covered terrace where the splashes of the tidal waves below create an atmosphere of being on a boat. It is most popular for the entire year, except for the two months with inclement weather. The entrance for the club members and their competing fighters is situated at the side of the building, adjacent to the member's parking area.

Goran parked his Audi Sport, as he referred to the RS 5, bought from the first bonus he had received being executive director of the Martial Arts Club's string of clubs, he had established with his family and a share taken by a friend of his father. He would only be referred to as John, a sleeping partner, his father knew from his school days. Goran left it at that as his father had been the major shareholder and although

Goran was running the clubs, he respected his father being taciturn about John.

He had a short briefing by his secretary, Elena, the buxom blond, who spent her free time racing fast cars on the local circuit. She seemed to be in a bad mood today.

"What's wrong Elena?"

"It's the bad weather forecast, besides we'll have a race coming on."

"You mean the third sports car race of the season?"

"Indeed. I am snowed under with the bookkeeping and the school events I have to visit my son's debut in the basketball team. "

"Well, I will see that the club members will support you and your son's basketball team."

"That would be great! Thanks Goran." She sent him a kiss.

"I have to go to the race track for a training session. Keep track of any calls."

Sure, will do."

"And enter me for the race in the senior sponsor section."

"Yes I will do it straight away. I am impressed."

"Well I am not one of the best drivers, but after all it's for charity." Goran left, wondering about Elena, who seemed to be edgy today. Must be the changing high pressure system, he thought as he drove from the club grounds.

Elena's phone rang. "It's me." She recognized Caltis' voice.

"What's up?"

"Is the coast clear?"

"Yes, it is."

"I'll be there in ten minutes."

"OK." Caltis hung up. Elena sounded strange today, with a slight angry tone. She must have problems with her son, who had been reprimanded for taking drugs at a school party. Well, my problems are mountainous compared to a drug related incident, he thought stepping from his car and entering the club building, with Elena's office located closely to the public entrance hall. He stepped into the general area that extended to the club members entrance. She heard him coming.

"Hey Caltis, what's up now?"

"Cool it there, you sound angry."

"I have tons to do here and in two hours I have to fetch my son from basketball practice."

"OK, this won't take a long time."

"Tell me."

"Mh," Caltis coughs, "it's about the upcoming race."

"What about it?"

"You have to participate."

"ME? I have no car, no sponsors and no entrance fee."

"I'll have that for you."

"Really, you are joking."

"No I am dead serious, listen to me. I know that you are a good driver, I have watched you compete. You have the edge to pass all your opponents. "

"Well, it depends on the opponents."

"This race is important for the club, as it's for charity and it's heavily backed by their supporters."

"Yes, I know, but what has that to do with me?"

"First of all I need you to win the race."

"Hah! Against Goran I have no chance."

"Yes you will have, with a little help from your friend."

"Iannis? Leave him out of this."

"No he is as important as you, my key players!

"Get to the point."

"You must convince Iannis to fix Goran's car so that it looks like a mechanical failure."

"You mean kill him?"

"No, just tamper a bit, so he has to give up the race in the final rounds and as you are number two behind him, you will be winning the race."

"You must be insane, look for another driver."

"I just want to draw your attention to the video clips I have as proof that you strangled a lover at a sex party"

"It was an accident."

"Yes maybe, but it looks like murder to me. At least the public prosecutor would reopen the case that had been dismissed with doubts. You slept with the judge!"

"Bastard, get out of here."

"All right your son and family would be amazed to see this."

"Dirty scoundrel" Elena hammered the chest of Caltis, who came close, pulled her close kissing her. He knew how to push Elena's buttons for an instant sexual reaction.

"Say you don't like it." Elena moaned as Caltis took advantage of her. He pushed her over the desk pulling her pants down. He knew she never wore underwear and loved anal penetration.

"You damned pig," she murmured, as Caltis enjoyed his raw sex with her, clasping her generous breasts.

"It's great with you Elena, like old times, remember?" She said nothing and went to the bathroom to clean up. When she returned, Caltis saw that she had red eyes.

"Look Elena it's for the best for all and nobody will really get badly hurt."

"OK, I'll do it, give me the car and the starter's money and I will take up training today."

"Good girl, how I love your bums!"

"Enough Caltis, if this is business then give me an undertaking."

"What?"

"Give me the original video from the party and all existing copies now."

"After the race."

"NO WAY!" Elena screamed. "You pig! First you rape me and then you hold me for stupid. FUCK OFF! "

"Come, on calm down Elena."

"I will, the moment you bring the tapes, the car and the money."

"OK, OK, I could not help to force you down, as I desired you."

"Keep your low talk to yourself. I am not your whore." Elena lifted the receiver and pushed the buttons. Hallo, she mimicked is that the police?" Caltis panicked and he cut the connection. "I will be here in a few minutes." Then he rushed off to enter the change rooms. Elena suspected that he might have the tapes in his steel cabinet where he kept his sporting gear. She thought about the risks involved and she would talk to Iannis to tamper Goran's car carefully, so he would avoid a fatal accident. That way she would come into fame, receive back the incriminating evidence and be finally free from an alp that hung over her head for many years. Besides, when she would get another sponsorship for sports car racing she would quit her job as secretary of the Martial Arts Club. She could never work for Goran any longer.

Caltis returned with the cassettes. "Which one is the original?" Elena snapped at him. "This one." He pointed at the silver casing. Elena took a CD marker and marked it.

"I will check them and then destroy them."

Here is the cash." Caltis handed over a packet of money he had set aside from his loan from Nasos. It will be a worthwhile investment for his large bet for the unknown driver Elena and her odds would make him rich and get rid of Nasos forever. He smiled. As the race was scheduled in a few days, he could hide out from Nasos until he had cashed his winnings. He smiled, a rush of adrenalin chased up his spine, like an after quake of emotions he felt, fucking Elena after a long time. Besides he had kept a copy of the tape incriminating Elena, just for insurance.

"Don't forget to bring the car."

"I will bring it within the hour." He departed. All seemed to go his way.

Chapter Six
Takis

Nasos paces up and down his office, swearing. "That damned bastard Caltis, I will kill him." He stops in front of his fridge, reaches for a tin and opens the can that releases a swooshing sound. Then he pours his favourite drink into a tall glass, watching the bubbles floating to the top. This caffeine drink will make him alive and alert his senses. A plan forms in his head. He sends a final warning to Caltis' mobile phone, as his calls remain unanswered. He checks his watch. School is over soon for Caltis' daughter Lucy. He heard from his sources that she will spend the next days at her girlfriend's house, daughter of Takis, a friend of Caltis. This would be a good opportunity to abduct her. He checks his arms cabinet and takes a bottle of chloroform, cotton wool and a towel. He has to be careful to seek the right moment to catch her, when she is least alert. He drives off and his phone beeps. John's voice sounds as he activates the hands free button.

"Nasos?"

"Yes."

"I take it from your last report that Caltis owes us money.

"Yes, his payment is overdue."

"What are you going to do about it?"

"I raised the interest as per agreement and gave him an ultimatum."

"And?"

"It elapsed today and he has not turned up with the cash."

"I have to talk to him." Nasos felt belittled in his own efforts to get his money.

"I have a plan to make him pay double."

"But no killings, Nasos."

"No, only if he is turning dangerous I will retaliate."

"Well, let's see if I can come up with another plan."

"I have it under control John. I can handle it."

"All right, but I reiterate, under no circumstances any killings. I do not need dead bodies in the vicinity of my neighbourhood."

"Ok John, leave it to me." Nasos takes his Nissan 4 x 4 Roadster and arrives at the school of Lucy and her friend and watches them leave, being picked up by Takis' wife. He follows the light blue Toyota until close to Takis' house, where he cuts the engine and remains in a low seating position, sipping on a tin of 'red bull', he always keeps in his car. He knows the layout of a standard suburban house and keeps vigil until the girls are alone. Takis and his wife emerge for an outing driving off with their Toyota. He waits for ten minutes and then opens the car door, places the chloroform, cotton wool and towel in his coat pocket and walks up to the house and checks the back door. It's open. He checks the windows and as he hears loud music on the first floor, he sneaks into the back door and moves to the phone. He checks the number and taps it into his mobile phone. He pours chloroform over the ball of cotton wool, activates a phone call and hides behind the staircase, close to the wall phone.

"I'll get it," Lucy's friend says and walks down the steps. At that moment Nasos moves like a cat from his hiding place and presses the chloroform mask above the mouth and nose of the surprised girl. Nasos places his arms below hers and moves her body around the corner behind the door to the basement.

"Rina?" Lucy calls out for her friend after a few minutes as she turns the music down. Hearing not a sound, she investigates walking down the stair. Nasos has renewed the cotton and towel wrap with more chloroform and is waiting for an opportunity to jump her. She stops at the wall phone to pick up the dangling receiver.

"Hello, anybody there?" Nasos slips and catches the unaware girl who turns, but Nasos has a steely grip to her throat. As she chokes he presses the cloth with the chloroform to her nose and mouth. Turning around her, he grabs her waist and continues with the chloroform until the girl is lifeless, He works feverishly strapping Lucy's feet and hands and then attending to Rina who has stirred. He applies more chloroform and then carries her body to the back door. He rushes out reverses his car to the driveway and opens the backdoor of his Roadster with enough space for two small children tucked away out of sight. For a good hour they will be knocked out. Time enough left to lock them up in the cellar of his house with enough amenities to serve as a perfect environment for the abducted teens. He has prepared a statement to send to Caltis and Takis, demanding first of all Takis' payment of interest and on top the ransom money for the release of the girls. He will issue instructions in due time. If he receives no response within 2 hours, one of the girls will be killed by a chance of draw.

When Takis and his wife Maria arrive home, they detect that the girls are gone.

"It smells like in a hospital," Maria says and Takis is alarmed as he finds no note and the lights on in Rina's room. "Chloroform," he mumbles, "the kids have been kidnapped!"

At that moment his phone rings and Takis listens to a taped message: We have the girls. If you want to see your daughter alive again, have

100 000 Euros ready within 24 hours. I will contact you again and NO POLICE!

Takis is desperate, where will he raise that kind of cash? He has to phone his friend Caltis immediately, but the mobile of his friend is busy and his landline is engaged too. "Damned! Maria? "

"Yes", she replies crying,

"Please give me a drink." Maria appears with a bottle of *tsipouro* and two glasses.

"What will we do?"

"We have to settle down and I will try getting Caltis on the phone." After a few glasses of the potent drink Takis has regrouped and he is looking for his handgun. "I will give hell to this bastard, I promise," he mumbles.

Takis dozes off after imbibing half a bottle of the clear spirit. His wife took a sleeping pill on his advice and went to bed. His phone rang and woke him from his dazing.

"Takis?"

"Yes Caltis, have you heard about the girls?"

"Yes and I have found out who the swine is."

"Tell me."

"Not over the phone."

"My place now," Takis said.

"Agreed. I will be there soon." Takis opened the entrance door as Caltis parked his Fiat in the driveway.

"Thanks Caltis, come in. We are in a pretty mess."

"Indeed, but we can deal with it."

"How?"

"Let's sit down first. I have brought a bottle of clear *tsipouro* spirit, that'll chase away the cobwebs of fear."

"Who is he?'

"It's Nasos that loan shark. He is getting back at me."

"Damned Caltis, why did you get mixed up with such garbage?"

"That's a long story. He wants a high ransom and we will get him."

"How will you get it?"

"I have a plan, let me work on it. If he phones in twelve hours and I am not back, tell him I am arriving with the ransom money and he should name a handover place."

"Ok Caltis, the life of our daughters is in your hands."

"Not quite. How much money have you tied up in savings, Takis?"

"Well I could raise about 50 000 within my family."

"Excellent, raise it! I will at least double it for you tomorrow, don't fear." Takis looked at his friend, his face expressed doubts. "I will explain it to you later. We will have a meeting with our core of army friends tomorrow, please inform your friends to be on stand bye. Cheers"

"OK, Takis said and downed another tot toasting Caltis."

He settled down after Takis had left and called his friend Chronis, the 'Timekeeper'.

"I will be ready he assured Takis.

Chapter Seven
Kathy

Kathy has been reading in her favourite photographic magazine about an article on Helmut Newton's new exhibitions, when her phone rang. "Is that Kathy?" the voice sounded familiar, but yet strange as if muffled. "Takis is related to you and you have a daughter with him." Kathy became instantly alarmed.

"Who is this?"

"Never mind who I am. We have your daughter Rina. She will be freed if you convince him to pay his debts due. Failing that it will cost your daughter's life."

"Who are you?" Nasos cut the connection.

"Damned," Kathy murmured, her brain searching all connections with Takis and her. She walked over to her drinks cabinet and poured herself a stiff scotch. Slowly she came over the shock and emotion and she tried to think logically. First she intended to let Goran know, but he had a race today and she would not bother him clouding his concentration. The she would have to contact somebody with military or police experience to help her. On intuition she phoned Takis, after all it was their daughter's life online. "Kathy?" Takis sounded under the influence. "I need to talk to you at my place. It's urgent." "OK, I will be there soon." She hung up. Takis arrived ten minutes later. He really drove hard, she thought. She let him in. He greeted her with a friend's kiss. He smelled of old potatoes. The fear in his perspiration, she thought.

"Takis, I had a strange phone call."

"Yes?"

"Rina had been kidnapped."

"Yes, I know."

"You know and have not told me?"

"Well, in the threats that I have received the caller kept telling me to be discreet about it."

"But it's my daughter too. "Takis appeared helpless. She offered him a drink, but he refused. "I had too many already."

"How do you intend handling this?"

"I have agreed a plan with Caltis."

"Caltis?"

"Yes, he will come up with the ransom money."

"Who are these guys?"

"His name is Nasos, related to the underworld."

"Aha, Mafia. How do we suppose to ever free our daughter from their clutches, you idiot?"

"I rely on Caltis and his action plan."

"What is his action plan?"

"I do not know until he pitches with the ransom money."

"If I am not informed at all times about all the movements, I will shout alarm and tell everybody I know, including the police."

"That's exactly the right way to execute our daughter and her friend."

"Her friend?"

"Yes, Lucy, Caltis' daughter."

"He has her too?" Kathy paused. Now I know what the story is all about."

"Well it's rather complex."

"Be prepared for help if you attack the kidnapper's holdout. I am willing to assist."

"Thanks Kathy."

"Chin up Takis, I used to be a crack shot at our outdoor sporting events, remember?"

"Yes, I taught you some of the tricks myself, coming back from the army service."

"Indeed. I am thankful for that." Kathy filled her glass again.

"Cheers," Takis said and prepared to get up and leave."

"Not so fast soldier," Kathy approached him. "It's our daughter's life that is at stake here and you have to promise me to do your utmost to save her."

"Promise." Takis replied.

"It's awfully hot here, don't you think?"

"Yes, I guess." Takis sensed his chance to top up on his funds he will have to hand over to Caltis for betting on the sports car motor race when he will leave in an hour's time. Kathy sensed Takis' attraction to her and she opened her blouse. As he came closer to her she kissed him. Takis could not resist her beautifully shaped breasts and her lithe body. He wanted to fall over her.

"Not so fast soldier," Kathy laughed. "Still have the hots for me?" She lowered herself opening his fly. He had an erection. He started talking as she began teasing him. "Kathy could you help with a bit of cash we could double?"

"Well," she said taking a breather. Maybe I have ten thousand I could bet. Tell me more about this bet. Takis told her what he had heard about a fixed race from Caltis.

"Do you trust him?"

"Yes, he has to double his money or he is dead."

"Sordid stuff. Let me treat you more." She increased teasing him.

"That would be great and…" he could not finish his sentence, as all became a blur. He closed his eyes as a leap of flame raced through his body. Then as he felt relaxed, his knees caved in.

"Take a sit Takis," Kathy said," I will be right back." She disappeared to the bathroom. Takis felt in heaven. Since days the unbearable tension had been lifted from him, which Maria could not do, but Kathy was a master in.

"Don't forget to inform me immediately of any new developments Takis."

"Yes love I will do."

"Now when's the race and what's it called?

"Today, the sports car racing by MAC members for charity. You must bet Elena for a win." Takis gave her all details. Kathy switched her TV on.

It was high time, as the betting had started on the pending sports car race and the odds were still high on an unknown driver, called Elena, Monroe of sports car racing, as a reporter called her in his radio interview. More interviews followed with drivers of the third local sports car event. Goran appeared shortly stating the good cause he was driving for. Susan appeared much to the surprise of her friends and the club members at the Martial Arts Club.

"Goran's interview had been short," Takis said.

"I guess that he was not pleased that Susan was competing against him."

"But he is number one spot anyway, according to the bookmakers."

"Yes, but it seems to affect him personally."

"Well, I eat my hat," Takis jumped up in his seat.

"What's that?'

"The odds are 30:1 for Susan winning the race. "

"Wow! Did you bet on her?" Kathy's question was affecting Takis like a shot.

"You bet we were."

"Do you know something that I do not know Takis?"

"Oh, I only know that Caltis has placed the bets."

"Gee", Kathy cried out, we will not make much betting on Goran for a win."

"No, but maybe Caltis knows more than we know about it. "

"Aha".

"Look at the money going on to Elena; they call her 'Monroe' of sports car racing."

"Indeed, her odds have dropped to 27:1 by now. Takis left he had to rest before the task ahead to free the girls with Caltis and his gang. He would have an early rest thanks to Kathy. He drove carefully home. .Kathy had phoned a friend at a betting office closest to her and she placed all her savings on a win by Elena. It went against her grain, but after all she did it to help freeing her daughter. Then she placed a phone call to Susan, but she could not reach her. She left a message for her soulmate to take a generous bet on Elena for a win.

When Takis arrived at home, the odds for Goran remained 8for 10, while for Elena winning the odds had dropped to 20 for one. A huge amount of money was riding on Elena for a win. He thought of the huge risks involved and the riches they all could make. Soon the race would be started and all would be over by the time when he woke from his snooze. He left the TV running.

Chapter Eight
Rina

Caltis had delivered the Audi Sports car RS8 in time for Elena to get acquainted with it, with the help of club members supporting Caltis. They had put up the guarantee and the hire-costs for the car. Besides as her boyfriend was the mechanic in Goran's stable and being part of the club, driving for charity, she enjoyed the same attention as all of them. She had trained hard for the race and soon she mastered driving the beautiful car to the satisfaction of her trainer, clocking best time unofficially. Alex, her trainer, a friend of Caltis advised her to stay in second position for the majority of the race and move only forward when Goran had some trouble and slowed down. But she would get orders by headset from her racing stable.

Meanwhile Caltis headed for the safe house of the windmill, he had agreed with Takis and his friend to meet after the race was over. Then they would cash their winnings, don their fighting gear and head for Nasos' stronghold residence.

When Elena felt that she could win the race even without the help of Iannis fixing the car of Goran, she asked her boyfriend for an evening out to a strip club, where she used to work before she met Goran. Iannis had checked her car over and found it in peak shape, locked it up in the safe cage and they drove to town in his new Alfa Romeo Spider, he received as a loan car from the sponsors of the mechanical back up team. He loved the car and Intended to buy it as soon as it became a special offer to members of his team. But Elena convinced him to invest in betting on her, as she was poised to win this race with a superior car, even if he abstained from tampering with Goran's sports car.

Iannis went to the betting office at the strip club and invested his savings of 20 000 Euros on a win by Elena. The day before Elena had betted most of the cash Caltis brought her, on a win by herself. She had received odds of 30:1 and this spurned her on to win at any cost. Iannis still received great odds of 27:1 and smiled as he returned to their table.

"I believe that you will win," Iannis comforted his buxom girlfriend. Her smile melted his heart and her low cut top showing off her pair of natural full breasts made her most desirable and attracted a following of many red hot pursuers. But she had only eyes for her Iannis, who appreciated her driving talents and who coached her with special tips and pointers, he heard from his colleagues in the racing stall. Besides the gossip about competitors yielded valuable inside information and detailed data of their respective driving skills and the status of their cars. While the pair returned from the dance floor and enjoyed their meal, Iannis observed a short man, looking like a dwarf with a hunchback accompanied by two bodyguards that towered over his every move, scanning the space constantly. They moved toward the lift at the back reserved for members of a gaming club upstairs. It was clear to Iannis that they were an underground set-up, who partook in a money laundering scheme, upstairs.

He had no idea that Nasos had a great scheme to bet a huge amount on a win by Goran and secure himself entry into the core of high stake gamblers at the heart of underground gamblers. Little did Nasos know about the workings at the sports car racing from members of the Martial Arts Club that Caltis had cunningly fixed with a risky venture. Their kidnapped girls were to be killed the following day, if Caltis missed to deliver the cash requested.

Nasos indicated a hand sign across his neck, as John asked him about the status of his two teenage hostages.

"You can't do that," John whispered to Nasos.

"You have us rather killed by the Don?" Nasos replied. John whispered back that he will approach the Don tonight, after their card game. Nasos found John going soft in his later days, once being a fierce street fighter for the Don. He has lost it, Nasos murmured and John sensed that Nasos would play him out against the Don. If he liked it or not, he had to get rid of the ugly dwarf.

The card game ended and Nasos came out even when he quitted, while John had lost a substantial sum, while he, Nasos, would increase his wealth at tomorrow's race. He gave

John a lift home and would not stay for a usual nightcap. He had been fed up with his partner's attitude, besides John had asked him to cook the books and he had to be careful to hide the red book before the next audit began in a few weeks. It would had meant his immediate death if the Don would have found about his cheating the organization through John for many millions. But he could never denounce John, he had to kill him. There was no way out. Then he could burn the red book and invest the money he had stashed away in a retirement fund on the Virgin Islands.

He smacked his lips thinking of the two girls in the basement. He would pay them a visit before he went to bed. Perhaps a few drops of cannabis extract would make one of the girls willing to play with his huge cock. He painted a fantasy world of sexual desires in his mind and felt happy like a lark as he arrived at his place, deactivated his external alarm and once entered, readjusted it for internal security for the night. Then he prepared the spiked food and served it to the girls in the basement. They received him with their usual moans and whining. Removing the duct tape from their lips, they started to fall about the good smelling stew and ate all up in a jiffy.

"You have been hungry my sweet children," Nasos sweet talked them to relax and be happy as their release would be the next day. Slowly the cannabis extract began to render the girls drowsy, but Rina was first to play along and fall for Nasos' sweet talk, hoping to escape. When Nasos became enamored as she opened her blouse to let him kiss her breasts. She rushed off and out the door running up the stair with Nasos hardly keeping up to follow her. But as she could not get out anywhere at the ground floor, she run upstairs, hoping to get out of the windows. He caught up with her and cornered her in his bedroom. "You were naughty and I was nice to you. Now you have to repent and be punished. She fell to her feet begging for mercy. He asked her to see what he had in his pants. Rina opened his fly and a huge cock jumped her way. First she got a fright, but then fascinated by her unusual first sexual experience she obeyed Nasos to play with it. As his penis grew harder, he encouraged her to give it oral attention.

"Think of it as a lollipop," he laughed and reclined on his bed as Rina got the hang of satisfying him. She nearly choked when Nasos climaxed, but she recovered, felt sick and rushed to the bathroom. She cleaned up and felt better. She tried opening a window, but it was impossible. Nasos inner security had been activated. She checked on the dwarf, who had fallen asleep on his wide bed and Rina raced down to the ground floor, looking for the main security board. She tried the red switch and a piercing alarm sounded, but she could open the doors to the lobby and the entrance. Nasos' guards had shift change and were caught flat-footed. Rina ran off like chased by a wild dog, she ran as fast as her feet would take her. The effect of the cannabis extract gave her strength and endurance. In a short while she spotted a cab and waved it down.

"TO THE TAKIS RESIDENCE! Hurry, it's a matter of life and death! She gave the cabbie the address. He stared at her breasts. Then she noticed that she had her top open and adjusted them. "Please phone this number now." She dictated the cabbie the mobile phone number of her Dad. He answered immediately.

"Takis, who is this?" I am a cab driver, I was asked..." Rina grabbed the phone.

"Daddy? It's me."

"Oh thanks god, where are you?"

"I am coming home with a cab."

"We will be outside waiting for you." Takis felt it was a trap and took his army pistol.

Then he positioned himself in a safe distance from the entrance of the house, asking Maria to stand close to the entrance door.

When Rina emerged from the cab and Takis saw that is was not a set-up, he ran toward his daughter and hugged her. "Please pay the cabbie," Rina said and Takis gave the man a note and thanked him, telling him to keep the change.

"Daddy you must go and save Lucy."

"First things first. Tell me the address where you and Lucy were kept.

"Who is the man?" Rina described him. " Aha Caltis was right. "Change your clothes and stay with your Mom!" Rina was comforted by Maria, who took her to the bathroom to clean up.

"'You smell terrible," she said, "time to have a good soak." Rina reflected upon her escape and the drug that made her do sexy things and then escape magically from her prison. She felt guilty about Lucy, who had fallen asleep. She could do nothing about it. At least now her father knew where to look for her and she would have helped at least for rescuing her.

Alarmed, Takis commanded his team to assemble. He would not miss an opportunity to hit Nasos immediately, while he was still under the influence.

Chapter Nine
Elena

The race participants assembled to a pre-racing get together after the last qualifying drives, where Susan had the best times, although only Goran's test times for the top spot had been released. Susan is upset, having opened up her talents to her trainer, who has been impressed with her performance, but had done nothing to correct the official time announcements. He rather has an eye for her well-shaped body, especially attractive in her tight fitting racing suit.

"I had the best time out there, Alex," she scolds his decision not to publish it.

"Yes, my racing Monroe," he teases her.

"When why don't I get the top spot?"

"Sorry Elena, I just adhere to racing orders."

"You are a faggot and intimidated by a bunch of hypocritical guys."

"Be it as it may. Just listen to me for a moment, before you shoot off your loose mouth." Elena purses her lips and Alex who has suppressed his true feelings, comes close to her. For a few seconds he controls his emotions.

"Please remove your headgear." When Elena removes it and her mane of golden hair flows freely onto her shoulders and on impulse Alex wants to stroke it.

"I have to whisper this into your ear." He swallows.

"OK Alex, I trust you." She can sense his vibrations.

"This has nothing to do with how I feel about all of this, please do not judge me."

"OK I will listen to you," Elena looks at him like a lost child. Alex's heart longs for her embraces, but he quickly controls his emotions.

"I am here because I am an expert on an advanced training for racing drivers, especially for sports car racing." Elena nods.

"Now, you have done extremely well in a short time and it is superfluous to say that you have talent" Elena smiles and she opens her protective racing suit. He gazes at her breasts, then concentrates and carries on.

"Now, we have a peculiar situation here. According to the rules you might have a case to put forward, but I would advise strongly against it."

"Why is that?"

"My dear Elena, let me remind you that you have entered this race on grounds of purely doing it for charity and it does not exclude unlicensed drivers, as you are at present."

"Oh, I did not know." Elena purses her lips and Alex is about to kiss her, but he holds back.

"Well, I think that at the end of this race today, you will have offers for a few contracts."

"Oh that would make me happy." Elena opens up her racing overalls revealing a sexy cat suit below. Alex is already highly besotted with her and wishes to touch her.

"Well," he rasps, "I will speed up the process of your racing license, but you have to promise me to act in accordance with our instructions."

"In that case I will. Don't worry Alex about this first spot, I can get there anytime."

"You are a darling and my favourite racing driver." Alex cannot hide his feelings and Elena senses her opportunity to completely encapsulate him erotically to her. She touches his face and strokes his chin. Alex embraces her.

"Not here Alex, the cams are on." He draws back. "Come here!" Elena takes a seat in the Nissan Patrol that has been provided as a transfer vehicle to members of the racing teams. Alex cannot believe his good luck to be close to Elena, he adores and venerates. She kisses him and he pushes her soft top up and enjoys kissing her full breasts. Alex is easily enticed and stirred, Elena observes and she touches him while she goes down on him. Alex is overly excited having pent-up emotions for her and he climaxes quickly.

"Ah Elena," he sighs.

"It's a thank you for all your hard work Alex, dear." She smiles as she rearranges her top and steps from the car. And now we are relaxed and have to join the pre-race party." Alex agrees and he is off to the change rooms.

Elena adjusts her racing gear and walks over to the assembly hall where most participants have already arrived. She takes a carbonated drink and meets up with Iannis, who lauds her performance. After fifteen minutes, she apologizes "I have to rest now." She lies down on the easy beds provided for the drives to rest. In her mind she concentrates about the circuit and replays her coach's comments seeing herself driving.

She is a true champion, Alex murmurs as he cleans up and slips into a new sports overalls. She'll is also a true Amazon. He smiles. No other woman has handled him with such an excited blow job ever. He will see to it that she'll win this race.

Iannis has watched Caltis and he has linked up to the cam that overlooks the rest room area of the racing pit ranges. Elena has lied down and she seems to have dozed off. It is necessary that she is physically and emotionally in top shape for the race. The mix of drivers and patrons, mechanics and race officials all enjoy the moments of the pre-race socializing. Then the siren will sound, all the visitors and sponsors have to withdraw to their seats and only drivers and racing staff will remain. Caltis has watched Elena and her trainer getting into the Nissan and he felt a bout of jealousy. However it is all for done for the course that she will win, he reminds himself. At that moment he saw Elena entering the restroom, Caltis followed her. He kept behind at first, allowed her to relax, but then he could not any longer stay in hiding and he approached her. Elena stirred when she saw him.

"What in hell are you doing here?"

"I thought of treating you to a nice drink, so you will be fully alert."

"Thanks but I do not need a drink."

"Then a few puffs of a joint?"

"Are you mad? I am in top form and I do not need a joint." Caltis realized that Elena was highly tensed up and he intended to relax her. This race was so important, she did not have clue how much. Besides there was enough time and more than an hour left.

"I came to calm you down," he approached her. Elena sat up in her stretcher bed. "No, just lie down. I will be nice to you." He touched her legs. "I will give you a good massage," he said softly. He knew she liked that.

"That will be nice of you, Caltis." She stretched.

"I will get a towel while you undress." He came back and Elena was already lying naked on her belly. "OK, I will start your favourite shiatsu," he said, placed the bath towel over her body and started with her toes. Iannis had established a link to the camera in the change and rest rooms, but he could not see what happened, only that the camera downloaded its observing content.

The social get together came to an end and slowly the people drifted away. Preparations of the mechanics began and soon the teams were poised for the start of the first race. By the end of the first race it was time to prepare Goran's car and while he appeared looking a bit nervous and irritated, Iannis observed that his laptop needed to be recharged. He quickly adhered to it and went back to his tasks of checking the engine.

In the change room, Caltis had lovingly massaged Elena and she had a climax resulting belatedly from her oral attention to Alex. It was unforced and it elated her, ridding herself from heavy thoughts and she thanked Caltis for not being selfish and taking advantage of her.

"I want you to be like a bird and fly to your victory," he said and kissed her. Strange, she thought, he had never been this gentle to her the entire years she had spent with him. Has Caltis changed?"

Caltis was satisfied to have kept Elena from being confronted with Goran at the pre-race gathering. He wanted her relaxed and without bad thoughts placed into her mind.

She emerged from the change rooms refreshed and smiling. Iannis said to her that she had never been as radiant as today.

"I am on a great ride today, Iannis."

"Indeed he said. I will be at your side."

"Thanks love. How's the car?"

"It's ready. Check it out."

The next race was announced for the sports cars, a race for charity and the participants were named. The signal came for the warming up of tires for a round and then for the drivers to take positions on their starting grids. All went well and Elena followed Goran who looked to her a bit under the weather. However, she talked to herself: concentrate on your own race. She weaved the car down the course and warmed up the tires fitted for her by Iannis. Some dark clouds had gathered and she noticed that he had taken care of fitting her car with all-weather tires. Her car felt great. Good handling and instant steering wheel reaction, with a good grip of the wheels on the road. That's how she liked it.

The starter called for taking their places. Her headphones seemed to crackle a bit, but it did not matter to her. Her heartbeat was normal; perhaps it soon will be a few strokes up after the start. She smiled. "Elena everybody loves you," she heard the voice of Alex through her headphones. Now for 1.5 hours she has to endure and be alert. It is the lowest range of sports car racing, but she could excel at this race and make a name for herself.

The flag fell and the start was off. Elena gained speed in her enthusiasm, but she kept her spot behind Goran. This pattern went on for the next hour and the positions did not change, except for the weather, when suddenly it started to rain. Goran was angry that he had to stop for a change of tires and Elena gained the lead. She kept going with an equally steady speed, challenged at times by competitors, but she fended them all off, especially as her driving style was harmonious with her car's performance and nobody could pass her, as she came out superior, especially with her technique through tricky bends. Alex had taught her well, she thought as she saw Goran challenging her again for the lead, with another 30 minutes to go. She thought that he must keep the challengers off, even slowing down, but as soon as Goran passed her coming out of a *Hairpin Bend*, she let him go, but sped up to follow him as he increased his speed, which left most other competitors behind. Directives from Alex were short and to the point. He lauded her driving skills and told her to stay at the heels of Goran until she would be instructed otherwise.

"I wish I could pass him," she replied back, "after all I am the driver with a real competitive car and I could pass him at the hairpin easily." But Alex instructed her to stay just where she was and that she was doing extremely well. With ten minutes to go, Elena started to get nervous.

"What's up Alex?" But Alex remained quiet.

"Be careful Elena!" Alex's voice screamed into her headphone.

Suddenly the dark clouds burst and rain made the track slippery. Just in front of her Goran's car moved into the infamous hairpin bend and did not slow down. He seemed losing control and his car veered off the track and hit the way-out area with a gravel surface on the track expansion for security vehicles, but his wheels seemed to turn at random and his car rolled over. Elena reacted instinctively passing him with a burst of acceleration, enough to take her out of a danger of colliding with him. Goran's car suddenly veered back into the track and hit another oncoming car. But the driver could steer it back onto the track, while Goran's car toppled over and lay upside down. After a few moments of stillness it started to burn. The rain had stopped and smoke filled the air.

The fire safety vehicle raced to the spot and extinguished the flames, pulling Goran from the wreck. He was immediately looked after by the emergency first aid ambulance and transported to the nearest exit from the track adjacent to the hairpin bend. The race carried on in spite of protests and had not been stopped, as the rescue operation did not interfere within the race track and the track surface had been declared safe for driving. The smoke cleared and a helicopter appeared and Goran was taken to the nearest hospital.

Elena saw Goran's car veering off, but she concentrated hard to pass his car and she thought of nothing else, switching her windscreen wipers on.

"Go Elena, go!" The track is all yours. The rain had as suddenly stopped as it appeared and she switched her wipers off. She pushed the accelerator down and the R8 shot like an arrow forward, as if a wild jaguar had been held back by supernatural forces, would suddenly unleash the animal's bursting powers. By the time she passed the scene of the accident at *Hairpin Bend* again, the site was clear, and Goran's car tainted black from flames, pulled to the side.

Elena felt a cold shower rushing up her spine. It had been agreed to stop Goran's car due to mechanical failure. Under those circumstances he would have stopped the car in the safe zone, stepped out and walked back to the racing stalls. But this looked like a serious accident.

"What happened to Goran," she asked Alex through her headset.

"He is alive, don't worry, and just step on it." Elena, saw the buildings around the finishing line coming up, the finishing line and the checquered black and white flag. She had not even realized that she had accelerated to top speed and she slowed down when she heard "YOU HAVE WON, YOU HAVE WON, SWEET MONROE OF CAR RACING." She heard the shouting of Alex and Iannis and others, but she was also aware that she had clinched only a pyrrhic victory. It has been completely unnecessary to tamper with Goran's car, as she would rather have preferred to beat him to the finishing line with the high adrenalin of sport like competition. She felt to be a victor, but she missed the real thrill.

Chapter Ten
Goran

Goran had felt uneasy the whole day before the race. He had to attend a budget meeting at the martial Arts Club boardroom and although income was greater than expenditure, the increasing trend for spending on maintenance had to be scrutinized. He encountered a hostile motion of extending the club facilities, as competition had added a specific youth section for membership and this club had to do the same. He saw that the motion had started with a drive by one of Caltis' friends, but he sensed that his opponent had been behind this for a purpose. As Caltis was not present the voting went in favour of his own veto, but then Goran realized the trend of driving a thorn into his flesh has started more aggressively through Caltis' men.

He had forgotten the rocky meeting and he had missed the pre-race gathering, but he was not in the mood for small talk anyway. As soon as he entered the racing track's registry office and fetched his badge, nothing mattered any longer but winning this race. Then he changed into the fire resistant racing outfit, but thought of placing the protective facial mask on at a later stage, as he disliked the tight fit around his head and face, which interfered today with his physical wellbeing. However, he thought not much about it further and resorted to the round of warming up his tires. He saw in front of him a new car and he recognized the red R8 Audi. As he came closer he noticed the familiar blond mane of hair protruding around Elena's face. I had no idea she would compete today, he murmured and checked with his racing marshal.

"Indeed, she has been registered and sponsored by Team C," the marshal said. "Where are they from?" Goran had never heard of them. "They are sponsored by members of the Martial Arts Club." Aha, Goran thought, it could only be Caltis' men and Elena had been set up by them. Well, she is a good driver, he mused and as the prize money goes to charity, she's welcome. Besides she has a brand new Audi, one notch up on his model. But whatever way the cookie crumbles, I will give her a tough race, Goran mused. Satisfied with his car, he moved to pole position on the starting grid.

The race, successfully started off, began with a scramble for places. Goran could maintain his position for the first rounds without anyone coming close to him. Mostly amateur drivers and without the stress of professional racing for high price monies, the competition seemed not to be fierce. However, just as Goran started to relax, he was leading and the red Audi was the only car chasing after him. The race order remained constant at the top for most of the time and an hour had already passed. Goran felt the endurance to clock the track ahead of the pack advantageous, albeit boring, yet something worried him about the steering through *Hairpin Bend*. However, 30 minutes before the end of the time limited race, the growling of a thunderstorm meant that the area would be hit by rain.

"Goran come in and change tires," his order crackled through his headphone.

"Why did they not fit all-weather tires in the first place?"

"It had been an oversight," Alex apologized.

"My steering has to be checked as well."

"Will do," Alex assured him. As soon as he drove into the area for a pit stop, Susan passed him. The tires, changed, Goran shouted to the mechanic, who raised his thumb for his steering to be OK. Cleared, and fitted with all-weather tires, he raced after Elena's red Audi. With a few rounds left he had passed Elena just before *Hairpin Bend*. He wondered why Elena did not make use of his pit stop and move ahead. His maneuver was risky, but it paid off. Feeling already victorious he pushed his accelerator to maximum speed with Elena hard on his tail, which irritated him. Suddenly a cloud burst and rain pelted down. His steering played up again and driving too fast into *Hairpin Bend* his steering ceased and his car shot into the opposite direction across a gravel area for emergency vehicles. That moment Elena passed him. He lost control and was hit by a car behind that sent him tumbling to the side and somersaulting against the barrier rail. Smoke filled the air and his car.

"I am on fire," he yelled into the headphone before he fell unconscious. The sudden rain stopped and as the fire engine had trouble starting their truck, it came later as usual. As every minute counted they arrived just in time to pull Goran from his wrecked car. His headgear loose, flames had caught his head and face. The first aid van worked with great efficiency and alerted the emergency helicopter on standby. It arrived minutes later on the helipad and Goran was flown to the nearest burns hospital.

Goran woke from a dream. He was flying through the air and parts of his car around him like in a silent, ghosting dance.

"I am burning, I am burning!" He shouted. Sweat ran down his eyes, which had miraculously survived the flames, but his facial skin had been roasted and disfigured him. Bandaged like a mummy, he felt as if he would be still incarcerated in his car.

"It's OK, I am here to help you," he heard the soft voice that reminded him of Kathy.

"I am glad you are here Kathy," he fantasizes. The nurse takes his hand and strokes it. This seems to pacify Goran, who had been immediately treated and after two weeks placed into a special recovery ward. His nurse, a young Englishwoman trained in intensive care, had nursed Goran through the worst, right from the start. A fan of his Tai Chi fighting, she promised to nurse him through to full recovery. As soon as she sat next to his bed, she held his good hand and he felt at times amorous, especially after a shot of pain killers. He talked in his sleep and started caressing her. He thought of her to be Kathy, his girlfriend. She loved the great sportsman, who had such bad luck racing for charity and she would let him touching her at night, when nobody was around. This erotic relationship increased as Goran became stronger and his burns began to heal up, thanks to his dedicated intensive care nurse. Dressing his half body, torso and face, demands patience and dedication, helping him with hydrotherapy meant to become intimately connected with his awakening body. Redressing him again with this constant routine had welded them emotionally together. But Anne had the gift of keeping an emotional distance, although she was here for Goran day and night.

Kathy visited him immediately and she was devastated to see him in such a helpless state. He thought that his accident had sealed the end of his career as a Tai Chi fighter. What would become of his clubs? His father was still in the chair, but he intended to sell his shares to finance his son's immediate recovery. Kathy noticed the presence of Goran's colleagues and club members. At one time she surprised Caltis and Elena, standing in the passage, viewing Goran through the window of the intensive station. They had not seen her coming and Kathy remained hidden to them at the door to the staircase. She heard Caltis talking to Elena.

"Well, I think he will not be able to come back to Tai Chi again."

"I think that I will win the next car race with the money I earned," Elena said.

"Now it's time to take over the reins at the club," Caltis said and Elena looked concerned.

"After all I cannot stay on as secretary!" Elena shook her head.

"We will see if you will be voted even into a higher position," Caltis replied."

"Let's go," Elena said, "I feel hungry." But she felt emotionally drained and guilty.

"Hungry for what?" Elena jerked back as Caltis moved his finger to her lips and asked that she suck it. Elena refused and left ahead of Caltis.

Kathy had a sick feeling in her stomach. When she approached Anne, she asked about Goran's progress.

"He comes on fine, Kathy. Don't worry by the time he leaves here he will be completely recovered." Kathy knew about Anne's dedication to nurse and care for Goran more than just with routine work, and thanked her. Goran had praised her and told her that thanks to her he will recover that much faster. He could already kiss Kathy and assure her that he loved her. Lately he had visits by the insurance assessors, who brought a specialist investigator from England, who had experience in accidents related to motor racing. As time went by there were rumors spreading through the club and also reaching Goran through his visitors. The questions asked by Mr Harvey, the investigator, pointed to the possibility of willful tampering with Goran's car. The evidence began mounting. Goran started feeling tense and he turned to Anne, who helped him physically to relax. She had against her principles fallen in love with him. It was high time Goran left intensive care and Anne knew she had to forget him, or apply for a transfer back to the UK.

Chapter Eleven
Kathy & Susan

Takis calls Kathy, but she does not answer her phone. Since Goran's accident she has no ears and no time for anybody else but sitting outside Goran's intensive care cubicle. Anne, the intensive care nurse looking after Goran, encourages Kathy to go home and sleep, before she will break down and be unable to attend to Goran when he is released from hospital.

Kathy has tried phoning Susan repeatedly leaving messages on her mobile phone. Susan is overloaded with work, as her partner Dr Wand had to attend a funeral of a close family member. Finally Susan answers her phone.

"Sorry Kathy, I have not forgotten to reply to your messages. It had been impossible up to now, but I will fetch you tonight, when I get home from the clinic." Kathy sounds deeply troubled and Susan senses she has to help her soulmate. "Will you wait for me?"

"Yes I will Susan."

At night around 11pm Susan rings the bell to Kathy's apartment.

"Thanks god you are here Susan." Kathy embraces her. Susan feels stirred but she realizes that she has to take care of Kathy, who is close to a nervous breakdown.

"Come with me Kathy."

"Yes, I will, just packed a few things." Susan takes her bag.

After a short drive Susan parks her BMW Roadster in her private garage adjacent to her clinic and helps Kathy with her bag. In the lift Kathy is overcome by emotion and she kisses Susan.

"Let's get into my apartment," Susan helps Kathy and locks the door behind them. Then she caresses Kathy, who is too weak to walk to her bed. She supports Kathy and let her lie back, removing her shoes and undressing her. Then she runs a bath in the Jacuzzi tub setting the temperature to a medium level. Then she drops her clothes and helps her friend into the Jacuzzi.

Kathy wakes up and embraces her friend. Susan is stirred and she strokes her friend's body and relaxes her. Kathy stretches into Susan who uses her hands to massage her soulmate's stressed body. Katy's feet curl around Susan's fingers and hand and she climaxes. Susan washes her gently and helps her from the tub. She towels her friend off and tucks her into bed. Then she pours herself a glass of red wine. She runs over a report and having finished her wine, joins Kathy in her bed.

The smell of toasted bread wakes Kathy. She notices that Susan had left. Aha, she thinks, breakfast time. She stretches and then recalls flashes of their lovemaking from yesterday night. Ah, the Jacuzzi had been especially stirring her libido. Susan is such a darling indeed. She dons a nightgown and walks toward the dining table in the nook close to the terrace, where Susan had opened the door. It is a sunlit area and the soft green and blue colours of the table cloth and serviettes enhance her appetite.

Susan, who woke early notices Kathy still sound asleep. Good for her, she thought, I'll prepare a scrumptious health breakfast: Fruits of the season and some soft boiled eggs, turkey slices and tomatoes, peppers and olives on fresh yeast free toast. She turns on the local radio station and soft music renders a magical atmosphere.

"Kathy" Susan approaches her as she walks into the space that interconnects lounge and eating area, kitchen and entrance hall.

"Susan!" Kathy embraces and kisses her. For a while the sweethearts caress, their silken morning gowns slip from their shoulders.

"You look beautiful Kathy," Susan says and kisses her nape. "Like delicious fruit, to be eaten instantly."

"I love to be eaten by you, love." Kathy replies and kisses her back.

"We are in great company, as we both reciprocate with great gusto." Susan says and she senses that sweet libido has scented their minds. "But first let's attend to our energies." She concludes. Kathy sits opposite Susan, her foot plays with her friend's leg. With every bite of food the lovers increase their desires and their libidos are soon aflame. "Come to bed," Susan coos and Kathy follows her. Kathy is speechless and she enjoys Susan's touches, her sensual ways to handle her erotic spots and her sense for French loving. She had phantasies about oral love before, but as it happened now out of the blue, it pulled her into its erotic ban and she sensed their perfect match with climaxing at almost the same time. Gasping, Susan moved up and embraced her soul mate. She could not utter a word and it was not even necessary. They both felt coiled up in the lap of heavenly pleasures.

Over coffee Susan approaches Kathy, as she senses that her friend needs to stay here for a while. "Kathy you need rest and some care."
"I have to be with Goran too."
"Sure, but give it time and patience."

"Susan, he has lost his looks, his face." Susan sighs and tears run down her face.

"Do not worry Kathy love; I will personally attend to it as soon as he is healed and ready for an operation." Kathy takes Susan's hands.

"Thanks Susan.

"Hey, cheer up, I will get him right."

"You think you can?"

"Sure Kathy."

"That sounds great! But how will we pay you?"

"Ah, Kathy. Remember the bet we took out on Elena?"

"Yes."

"Well we have made quite a packet, thanks to you."

"But it's dirty money."

"But it pays for all the medical care he will need to get 100% again." Kathy remained silent and sighed.

"If it all would have not been engineered..." Kathy sighed again.

"Well, let's leave that to the investigators to find out. Besides that might be a case to watch in the near future."

"What do you mean?"

"Well if it was an attempt on Goran's life, he can sue the culprits for compensation."

"I see, indeed."

"It'll come eventually right for Goran again, he is a fighter.

"I have to run to the clinic now, feel at home. If you want to go out, let me know. I will deactivate my system to let you out and in again. Here is the access card, a visitor's card you have to use after I tell you."

"OK Susan I will stay indoors, I have to catch up on sleep."

"OK, phone on this cellphone, I leave it here." Then Susan left in a hurry, satisfied that her friend and love interest felt already better.

Chapter Twelve
Nasos

Nasos is devastated. When he heard the news that Goran had an accident and lost the race two laps before its ending, his first thought was to wrap up his business and clear out of town, disappear from the clutches of the Don. John the Caesar owed a substantial amount to the king of underground and Nasos had invested heavily on John's order. Yet if they came for John, also his life would be on the line, as he had cooked John's books. It meant executions.

He rushed to his office and packed some handguns, a rifle and a shotgun, ammunitions and a bullet proof vest. He emptied his safe and left everything else behind. Then he initiated the self-destructing mechanism for an implosion, whenever the entry would be forced to his offices and left in a hurry.

His cellphone rang, but he ignored it. Driving along the highway to his house, he realized that he had left Lucy the teenage daughter of Caltis without food and water. She would be sleeping anyway having been introduced to cannabis. By now his whereabouts would be known to Caltis through Lucy's friend Rina, who had miraculously escaped, as his guards had been asleep.

"Damned little bitch," he swore between his teeth. "I have to blow up the house, if they come for me!"

Caltis had moved with his ex-army buddies close to the vicinity of Nasos' residence. "We have to split up," he directed his four men to approach the house from different directions. "Watch his garage and the front door." The men moved out, in a wide circle, watching the landscape and use shrubs for cover, approaching the house carefully with weapons ready.

"There must be no shooting in case he holds Lucy as a buffer," Caltis' voice sounded through their headphones." The men confirmed. Caltis and Takis approached the back door of the residence and Takis signaled Caltis the approach of a guard. Caltis took his laser gun and aimed at the guard's head. He pressed the trigger carefully and after the dull swooshing sound the guard fell to the floor. Takis rushed to grab his legs and pulled him behind some shrubs. The friends took cover as the second guard appeared. Takis took him out and pulled him aside. Suddenly the Jaguar of Nasos turned the corner from the driveway heading for the garage. It was too late for Takis to turn back, He ducked and headed for the door, to reach the corner and enter the garage before it closed, but he slipped and rolled to the side of the entrance door. "Damned," he swore.

"We have taken out the other two guards," he heard through his headphones.

"Takis back me up," Caltis said, "I am going to try the window on the first floor.

"Caltis climbed the garage outdoor building and walked across its ridge of its roof to the nearest window. The casement window was slightly pulled up and obviously Nasos had forgotten to secure it, or he had switched off the alarm and had not activated the internal circuits yet. He pulled the window up, and stepped into a bedroom.

"Takis be ready to strike through the main entrance and the back door on my command!" Takis confirmed. The door to the room was ajar and as he tiptoed close, he saw Lucy lying in bed. She was asleep. He continued to her bed and placed his hand over her lips, when he woke her. Lucy stirred and wanted to shout frightened that the dwarf wanted to jump her.

"Quiet Lucy." She recognized her Dad. "Listen carefully: wait until Nasos checks on you here, when play him along a bit until I grab him. Then rush down and deactivate the alarm and switch off the main red switch "

Nasos had been busy to load his Nissan 4x4 with the bootie and forgot to switch the inner alarm on. He heard some strange noises on the roof and alerted the guards. Takis took the beeper from the dead guard and answered. "It's all right we will check it out," The voice on the other end sounded to him unfamiliar, but he let it go. He rushed to the entrance foyer and activated the inner alarm. Then he hurried up the steps to check on the girl. She lay in bed sleeping. When Rina had run away, he left Lucy, who seemed to be knocked out by a higher dose of cannabis, sleeping. Nice, he thought a quick little pleasure would heighten his spirits. He came close to her bed and he pushed the cover aside. His hand moved along her lithe body. Lucy moaned

"After all you are alive and had a nice dream." He stroked her cheeks and bend down for a kiss. At that moment Caltis threw a cord around his neck and pulled him back. "YOU DIRTY BASTARD. Leave my daughter alone! Nasos choked and tried to weasel out of the noose. "Run LUCY, you know what to do!" Caltis shouted and Takis already stood by at the entrance door, with two of the gang at the back door.

"I pay you back all your interest, let me go." Nasos screeched between his teeth.

"You dirty prick; I will cut it off now."

"I give you double," the dwarf negotiated, but Caltis held him tightly.

"I want to know where you keep your money." The dwarf whined, but Caltis throttled him. The door opened and Takis entered. He helped Caltis to tape his hands behind his back and kicked him repeatedly.

"You touched my daughter; you dirty swine, now I will cut it off!" He took his hunting knife and cut Nasos' waist button off and pulled his pants down. Nasos pleaded for his life, but Takis had built-up such an anger he cut his underpants open. His huge penis hung between his thighs. Takis placed his knife to his balls and a trickle of blood stained his white underwear.

"Wait, he pleaded, I will tell you everything. Please take the noose off. Caltis slackened the cord and Nasos told them the combination to the safe.

"Watch him," said Caltis and rushed out the room, embraced Lucy, in care of a team member. "Search the house and the cars and seize all weapons and valuables. The team rushed in all directions, while Lucy stayed with her Dad, who found Nasos' safe and opened it. He whistled. Stacks of money in various denominations were amassed here. Lucy helped him to load all into his knapsack.

"Cars are approaching," he heard the voice of his lookout. "Damned must be his underworld buddies.

"Let's clear out now. Come Lucy. All back to base." The gang rushed from the house, carrying knapsacks with weapons and ammunition, valuables and the bags from Nasos' car. Caltis could not see Takis and he wondered where his friend would be. As soon as flames leaped from the windows Takis appeared at base, behind cops of trees, exhausted. He had to run for his life to escape from the men entering the house. The gang doffed their fighting gear and remained in their civil clothes they wore below. Once they were safely at their cars and drove in a circle around the posh northern suburbs, they felt safe. Lucy leaned against her father's shoulders and fell into slumber. Takis' friend had given her a sedative. The men arrived at the windmill and prepared for a celebration. Takis warned them that they could be followed and should stack the bootie in the floor below, behind the grinding stones.

Chapter Thirteen
Elena

Elena and Iannis became suddenly rich. They have moved into a new apartment in a trendy suburb. Iannis stops her as she unlocks their new home.

"Wait. It is custom that even a future groom has to carry his bride over the threshold." Elena is surprised that Iannis has spoken for the first time of marriage and she becomes stirred as she lifts her up and carries her into their new apartment. He turns and kicks the door closed and takes her to be bedroom. She pulls him down on top of her and they roll on their wide bed. Iannis cannot resist touching her and soon his embraces inflame Elena's passion and they make love languidly at first. Filled with insatiable energy the couple cannot get enough of each other.

"My gorgeous lover Iannis, she coos endearments into his ear.

"I will love you to death," he whispers back.

"No Iannis, how, can I love you if you kill me with your love?" They banter and Iannis enjoys Elena's erotic powers that come with a series of her climaxes, he enjoys, holding back until he will join her with his own much later.

"You are my virile Iannis," she praises him, how could I ever let you go?"

"Don't!" He sighs," 'never let me go." Susan feels in heaven and falls into a relaxing sleep with Iannis' breathing tickling her neck.

When she wakes she stretches and yawns, gets up, dons her nightgown and walks straight to her new kitchen. She had selected it to her needs and Iannis has agreed that she should have free hand in selecting a kitchen with all trimmings and decorate the flat, besides choosing all the furniture and furnishings. She hums a song and prepares her late morning's breakfast. As she serves her eggs and tomatoes with green tea, she picks up the note left by Iannis. "Had breakfast, had a call to attend to a Jaguar for a client. See you soon. Iannis." What is he doing out early morning? A new client? He never told her about preparing a car, besides there are no forthcoming races for a while and he never mentioned a Jaguar. Elena has a bad feeling at the pit of her stomach. Since the tragic accident of Goran and her subsequent winning of the race for the Martial Arts Club, she had a steep climb from receptionist to club secretary and shareholder. It supposed to have made her happy, but when the initial thrill wore off, she felt a bad conscious of having been part of the conspiracy against Goran that had been described to her to be harmless, but nearly cost him his life. Goran had been badly burned and she felt responsible for causing it. When she was alone, she cried at times to relief the tensions that were building up in her, especially when she faced the dusky Caltis, who looked at her with preying eyes. Since Goran's accident she avoided him and excused herself from being alone with him. "I am engaged now to Iannis, she would utter. "Keep your hands off me."

Caltis pursued her and wanted her oral attentions to satisfy his needs, but she became repulsed of the dark man and began to hate him. She intended to talk to Iannis about her feelings. Although the heinous deed could not be reversed, and Goran's face could not be put back to his former dashing looks, something had to be done to get her conscious to be cleared. Iannis had been away for a long time and he usually phoned her when he was on his way home.

The ringing of her telephone startled her. "Iannis?"

"Alex here."

"Hi Alex what's up?"

"I am afraid it's bad news."

"What?"

"There was an accident."

"Iannis?"

"Yes, he is dead." She could not hear any longer Alex's explanations about the accident. She sensed from the pit of her upset stomach that he had become the next victim of the underworld. She had picked up a conversation at the club, linking Alex to the Don, a powerful gangster boss. She felt sick and ran to the bathroom, the receiver dangling to the floor. She had to wretch, kneeling down and placing her head above the bowl.

When she felt better, she straightened up from her kneeling position and cleaned her face. The cold water revived her. She poured herself a stiff brandy and drank it in one go. The warmth spread through her body and the colour returned to her face. She had another tot and her stomach stopped cramping.

Her telephone rang and she was afraid answering it. But when it rang again after a few minutes, she lifted the receiver cautiously.

"Elena?" She recognized Kathy's voice.

"Yes."

"Can you talk?"

"Yes."

"Susan wants to have word with you."

"Yes." Her monosyllabic reply worried Kathy and she told Susan.

"Hi Elena, are you all right?"

"Yes." She sounded stronger and had suddenly recovered from her shock of losing Iannis.

"I would like to have a word with you later if you are available."

"I am at home. I have to finish some tasks."

"OK, I will fetch you early evening, say seven?"

"Yes, that's fine." Elena's tears were freely running down her cheeks. She had abandoned the receiver and ran to her bedroom falling into bed overcome by a crying attack. She let go, slowly at first and then she fell asleep.

Susan heard her initial crying and became concerned that something tragic had happened to her. Hopefully the gangsters had not yet closed in on her, she thought. Kathy advised her to hurry and be on time. Goran had told her once that when something happened to them they would fall back on Elena, as she had blood group zero and wherefore she was a sought after person in emergencies.

When Elena woke again she realized that she had thirty minutes left to get ready. Susan was already on her way to fetch her. She wondered what it might be that she was important to her.

She knew from Kathy that Susan was her friend, a surgeon. While she applied some make-up and combed her hair, her doorbell buzzed. She released the entrance door and Susan entered.

"Hi Elena, I am Susan,"

"Nice meeting you. Please come in I am soon finished."

"You have a nice place here."

"Yes it supposed to be Iannis' and mine."

"Is it not any longer?"

"No, he is dead! He was killed this afternoon." Elena looked at Susan and tears rolled from her eyes.

"I am sorry Elena." Susan hugged her. "Tell me," she said.

"He had to prepare a car for a client and he seemed to be late for coming home. Alex phoned me and explained to me that his car exploded on the track."

"That is horrible. What type of car was it?"

"A Jaguar sports car. But I think it was no accident. Iannis used to be careful."

"Well, Elena, I am sorry, maybe we could look into it for more detail."

"I want to leave," Elena blurted out.

"We need you Elena," Susan said.

"What for?"

"I have a patient who needs urgently a blood transfusion."

"Can't you get supplies?"

"NO. And he is blood group zero."

"Oh I see, how do you know that I am the same group?"

"Because I heard from your former employer."

"Ah, from Goran?"

"Yes." Slowly Elena could form a picture in her mind. It dawned on her that it was an opportunity to make good and at the same time get help from Susan.

"Let me think about this."

"You may Elena, but I have to tell you that it's urgent. "

"OK, I will do it if you could help me too." Susan looked surprised.

"Of course."

"I would need a face job as I have to disappear before the gangsters get hold of me."

"Ok we will discuss it while I drive."

"OK," Elena sighed.

Feeling a sudden intuition popping inside her, Elena suddenly felt a way forward as a huge rock had been removed from weighing down on her. She could relive her debt to Goran and in exchange she could live under a new identity. Her confidence level started rising and her eyes sparkled.

Susan noticed a change in Elena's body language, as if she would have been touched by a magical wand.

Chapter Fourteen
Susan

Don's men enter the building where Naos' offices are located. As they feared a trap, they summon John, Nasos' partner. It is late afternoon and the twilight provides an eerier atmosphere. The air smells of decayed potatoes.

"Go ahead John, find us the books." The burly head member of the gang pushes his gun into John's back. John sensed that Nasos might have hidden the red book at his house, as agreed, but the house had burned down and there is no longer any evidence. He smiled, Nasos had been a crafty figure and now he is dead. He wondered what had happened at his place in a battle of a revenging friend whose daughter he held hostage and possibly had been molested.

John unlocked the door with his security key and reversed the alarm system. Suddenly he saw the books. Don's gang stormed into the other office of Nasos, where the weapons cabinet stood open. John grabbed the books and hid the red book by placing it onto sticky gum below the drawer of the desk.

"It's here" he said and the stocky guy came over and took the book.

"Where's the other one?" John panicked and touched the remote in his pocket.

"Which other one?"

"Don't play dumb with me, I saw you open the drawer." John pressed the overriding button on his remote that reactivated the alarm. The red light appeared and while the gang searched for the red book, John walked silently to the door and stepped out into the passage. Five seconds left, he murmured and ran down the stairs, rushing into the open and cowered behind a parked truck.

A huge implosion shook the building, blowing out windows and pulling down the entire upper floors. Debris scattered around the pavement and the roads, but most of the damage had been internal. John got up and walked to the nearest park, across which he knew of taxis always parking there.

The cab brought him to his house and he rushed to open his safe to take a few passports and money, donned a false moustache, a reversible coat and took his hat and pipe. Then he started his old fashioned BMW motorbike and drove towards the harbour at Piraeus.

Susan had driven Elena to the hideout area which is part of her clinic, separated with a secure entrance. Elena is impressed by the modern Hi-Tec facility and she is asked to lie down in one of the cubicles, while a nurse attends to take her blood. She feels drowsy after the procedure and falls into a relaxing slumber. Goran has been prepared for the facial operation. Dr Joachim Wand has prepared the matching facial piece from a young man killed in a car accident. The computer tests showed a perfect match to Goran's face with excellent medical comparative structure and skin type. Having done similar operations on an ongoing basis, Susan has trained her team to utmost efficiency. Susan's blood is helping Goran to stay fit and replenish the lost blood he suffered from his injuries. The operations is ongoing for most of the night, as Susan's specialist surgeons called on in an emergency have specific knowledge of rejoining tear ducts around his eyes and connecting the main nerves and blood vessels of the new facial tissue. When Susan dissects the scarred face of Goran, she is relieved to see his new face already placed onto his old face left without skin and tissue. She only relaxes when she is done, specializing in connecting the nerves and muscles around his lips, controlling the movements of lips and mouth, nose and surrounding areas.

"Skilled microsurgery at its best," Dr Joachim praises her and Susan lauds her team. In the early morning hours she pays back an earlier compliment to her partner Dr Wand. Meanwhile Elena has washed and cleaned, slipped into a gown and wheeled into an operating theatre where Dr Wand reshapes Elena's facial tissues, marked up with drawn lines on her face, as he and Susan agree on the way she would look best, changed enough not to be recognized as Elena any longer. Finally, after Elena is satisfactory under narcosis, he takes over and creates a new looking Elena. Susan works on her ears and lips. When the team is satisfied, they hit the showers and leave the patients in the care of their trusted nurses at the intensive care station.

Susan is welcomed by Kathy, who has prepared breakfast for her team. Dr Wand stays on with one of his colleagues, the others had already been booked for new appointments and having had coffee and some croissants they have to leave. Susan accompanies them to the lift and thanks them to have come at such short notice. She returns in high spirits, as both operations were successful, although she worried about Goran most of the time.

"Thanks Kathy for preparing such a scrumptious breakfast."

"My pleasure Susan, you and your team earned it and much, much more."

"Ah yes," Susan smiles, "I can think of something right now!" She hugs her soulmate. Their embraces become more intimate and Susan takes Kathy to bed. The sweethearts embrace and make love languidly. The pleasure is sweet and yet short lived.

In the middle of night Susan wakes from a dream. It is Goran! Somebody had bypassed the security system and entered the secret chambers of her clinic, where she keeps high profile people who wish to be undisturbed from news and reporters. It reminds her of Kathy's friend, who helped with the assembling of the mercenaries. She switches her bedside light on and notices Kathy missing. She panics, gets up and finds Kathy in her lounge, cowering in an easy chair sipping a drink.

"Kathy?"

"I could not sleep, worrying about Goran."

"He is recovering, Kathy, don't worry love."

"But I am worried."

"I am having a shower and then have some coffee, before I check on Goran."

"OK, I will make you coffee, meanwhile take your shower."

The intensive care nurses report good news to Susan that both patients are well and stable, receiving their nutritional and medical drips as prescribed by her. She checks the monitors and all seems to be just fine. A strange noise alerts Susan. Checking the security monitors for the perimeter fence reveals an intruder.

"Who the hell is that?" Susan points to a masked man overcoming the second fence. Susan calls security but there is no answer. Alarmed, she calls on Greg, the mercenary leader and he responds immediately.

"We have an intruder here at my clinic, Greg."

"On my way! Stay calm and lock all internal doors."

"Damned," Susan says and notices that security had been tampered with. It must be an inside job. She locks the clinic's doors with the over-riding switch from her cellphone and then re-treats to the secret area of the clinic securing the doors and keeping vigil at her patients, until Greg will arrive.

Chapter Fifteen
Susan

Caltis has instructed Takis to break into Susan's clinic and capture Susan in order to force Goran to hand over his shares in the Martial Arts Clubs. He does not realize that Goran had been operated on and Takis breaks the security system with the help of a night nurse, who is a friend of his wife. He cuts a hole into the first fence and he climbs the palisade at the second security, as the electric feed is cut off.

As he tries to get over the top somebody shouts "Stop right there or I shoot!" He freezes with hands up, legs on either side of the fence, the palisade's pointed edge cuts into his jeans and hurts his balls.

"I am hurt!" he shouts.

"Come down slowly and no tricks." Takis climbs down and raises his hands. Greg's men handcuff him and one chap takes him to the armoured van. An alarm sounds as Taki's men enter the clinic forcefully, using welding gear to force an entry. Greg rushes to the entrance commanding his men to shoot indiscriminately. A battle ensues and Greg's men can overcome Takis' gang. Three are down with one wounded guy trying an escape. Greg takes his rifle and shoots him. Then they signal to Susan who opens the inner door. As he enters the security guard's office, he finds him shot. "Send me an ambulance, security officer down," he yells and Greg's man, guarding Takis, phones immediately. The siren howls as Greg signals to Susan to be allowed to enter.

"Thanks Greg you came just in time."

"We have a warzone here, right at the threshold of your clinic."

"The alarms and security are compromised." Susan gasps, still shocked from the gun battle.

"The security guard has disappeared."

"He has been shot, I asked for an ambulance."

"We could look at him here." Sue replies.

"No, you have enough on your hands."

"I need the electric fence and the alarms reinstated."

"I'll send you Bill, he'll fix it for you just now. Karl, his right hand man will guard your clinic entrance until you find another trusted security man."

"Thanks Greg."

"My pleasure, at least we have a prisoner." He smiles.

"Who is it?"

"I believe his name is Takis." Susan sighs.

"He is the right hand of Caltis." Susan looks frightened.

"We'll take good care of him Ma'am."

"Thanks again." Greg had commanded his security expert and his helper and they tend to the damaged door, reinstall the alarm and test the repaired fence. All seemed to be in good order again. Susan is relieved. She hurries back to her patients. They are fine. There is hardly any noise from outside penetrating into her secret chambers. Even gun shots will be muffled to a great extent. Susan questions the night nurse,

"Have you noticed anything out of the normal last night?"

"Not at the beginning, but later the new young nurse, who came here yesterday for the first time, asked me to replace her while she went out for a smoke break."

"What time was that?"

"About five in the morning."

"Thanks, I will deal with her." Susan leaves having given her trusted nurse strict instructions. She must stay and let nobody in until she will return. A sudden tiredness comes over Susan. Damned Maria, she has to check out the young woman who helped Takis and his men to break into her grounds.

Greg and his men take Takis to their safe house and Kurt, Bills, right hand man occupies the security office and reinstates the communication board. He is satisfied that all observation cameras work and all connections are safe and telephones are in working order. Finally Susan retreats to her private lift and enters her safe-house apartment. Kathy has prepared a vegetable stew. It smells lovely and she welcomes Susan, who collapses into an easy chair. "What happened?"

"You don't want to know Kathy."

"Well, tell me! You look drained."

"It started off with waking to a nightmare, which I brushed aside, but when I heard some gun shots and someone forcing the Steel doors open to the clinic, I feared that my nightmare had started to come true."

"My god! Is Goran all right?"

"Yes, thanks to Greg and his musketeers everything is back to working order and it seems that the leak to Takis had been from one of my nurses."

"Takis?"

"Yes, Greg caught him and took him to his safe house to lock him up."

"Bastard Takis, what is he trying?"

"I have no idea, probably he wanted a hostage."

"A hostage?"

"Think Kathy, he is Caltis' hatchet man and Caltis wants Goran's shares of the business, so?"

"He wanted to kidnap YOU!"

"Bravo Kathy, you bright cookie! "

"Well come here give me a kiss." They hug. "This feels good." Susan is overcome with emotion and she starts sobbing. Her head rests on Kathy's shoulders.

"Just let it come out Susan." Kathy strokes her hair and kisses her head. The last 24 hours had been a grueling test for Susan and this attempted break into her clinic played heavy games on her nerves. Kathy held her tight until she caught herself again.

"You must eat something Susan. I have made a veggie stew and we have homemade bread with it."

"Super!" Susan beamed, "what are we waiting for? Let's eat!" She had regained her composure and just after some spoonful of Kathy's stew she was again her usual self.

"It's delicious Kathy. My! How I love this stew and your bread."

"Let's have some wine." Kathy poured the golden drink into Susan's glass before she filled hers.

"This wine complements the food Kathy. What is it?"

"Golden Chardonnay."

"How exquisite," Susan lauded her. They ate in silence and Kathy let Susan finish toasting to her.

"All the best to your patients, may they have a speedy recovery and congratulations to you for a great job!"

"Thanks Kathy. There will be still work that has to be done. But I am confident that all will be just right." Susan smiled again and her skin glowed. Kathy stood up kissed her cheek and took the dishes to the kitchen.

"Let's have a shower together, relax and watch some news." Kathy winked at her.

"Yes, that's great, but before we do that may I ask you for a favour?"

"Sure, anything." Kathy said.

"Could you contact your journalist friend George and ask him to check out the background of one of my nurses?"

"Sure. What's her name?"

"Maria Koreas."

"I heard that name before," Kathy replies and dials George's direct number, while Susan re-filled their glasses...

Chapter Sixteen
Caltis

Caltis has won the local championships and has qualified for the European Masters Championships in Paris. With Goran out of contention, he had also engaged his friends and former army buddies to help drumming up support and through interconnections to influence the jury. His team had celebrated his victory and the raid on Nasos' residence had netted him a great deal of cash he wisely invested into the martial Arts Club, buying up any share he could lay his hands on. A few percent of the shareholding separated him from becoming chairperson and owner of the chain of clubs. Already his income soared and he had a good adviser in Takis. He had hoped to force Goran to sell his shares for a nominal value, as he reckoned that the unfortunate competitor had enough trouble to get his life together again. He was assured that Goran was in need of funds to pay for his hospital bills. Takis had found out that Goran had been supported by Kathy and that Susan had taken him into her private clinic in order to reconstruct his face. Takis had planted a nurse, called Maria, a friend of his wife, who had been educated in England and he intended to use her for inside information. By the time she had been accepted to report for night duties, Takis gave her instructions to take photographs of the switchboards for security. His internal connections to a member well versed in electronic security and alarm systems designed a plan, simplified for Maria to switch off the security and alarm systems to allow Takis to gain access to Susan's clinic. But the plan backfired. He knew that Goran had treatment there, but he had no idea about the details, besides the secret wards of Susan's clinic, were impenetrable. Takis could advance as far as the entrance area, having overcome two security zones, but then a group of professional trained soldiers caught him. It must have been Goran's men, but where did he draw on such funds needed to keep a private army? Caltis smashed his fist on the table of their safe house, where he had ordered all the remaining gang members for an urgent meeting.

"Takis is held captive. You must find out where he is. Do not attempt to free him, as our opponents are professional soldiers." There was stillness in the room, the smoke of cigarettes rose toward the top floor, where the skeleton of the unknown woman still hung from the roof beam. A scent of decay wafted at times toward them mixing with the acrid smell of cigarette smoke. Caltis continued after a pause. "So prepare for doing good intelligence work while I am gone to the championships. I expect a detailed report by the time I am back. It is only for a few days, so be on the constant lookout."

Chronis will be accompanying me and is responsible for security in the absence of Takis."

Chronis whispered a name into Caltis' ear and

the gang boss nodded. "In our absence Castor will be leading you." Caltis instructed Castor and his gang and referred them for advice to Alex, who reported to him directly. They ran through the tasks again and Chronis summed it up: Surveillance of all subjects as per list, searching for the whereabouts of Takis and securing all data of the place and its surroundings, typing of reports and posting it on the secure Internet site, consulting Alex in times of duress. Besides you have to keep away from this safe house, but monitor anyone coming close through the video cameras." The meeting was officially closed and Takis and Chronis left to rest before their journey. Castor was responsible for locking up.

Charles de Gaulle airport with its central circular tower is an impressive entry into the great city of Paris and its spectacular space, filled with coming and going of passengers, which amazes even the regular traveler each time. Caltis and Chronis and their assistants were welcomed by the official bus service for the competitors and VIP's of the forthcoming championships. Tai Chi had many enthusiastic followers in France, especially in Paris, where many Chinese and Far Eastern expats had found a second home. Caltis' father spoke French, but he had neglected the language. However as Chronis had a basic knowledge of French, and listening to him talking it, brought back the language to Caltis' memory and he enjoyed hearing the familiar sounds and phrases, without having to reveal his knowledge of it. This served Caltis' means to make valuable contacts through his comrade-in-arms, while he could concentrate himself on the pairings and competitors he had to face.

As soon as they arrived at the hotel close to the competition halls, Chronis attended the briefing seminars, while Caltis joined the training camp to rehearse his movements. Caltis worked hard, but he realized that competition was fierce, with scholars from Phelan, the famous British trainer and champion and from the schools of Sitan Chen, world famous and known as the Prince of martial arts. Having initially observed competitors, Caltis sensed that he could not win this championship and dark thoughts crossed his mind. He missed Takis, who had become the master of his dark thoughts and of their execution. Takis had many tricks up his sleeve to engineer always an advantage in competitions. But now Caltis had to rely on Chronis and although he was like a carbon copy of Takis, he lacked the same determination. He became easily distracted, especially by pretty women and always behaved well mannered, gregarious by nature. His friends had nicknamed him 'Micro Onassis' as he exposed a similar character of cunning, hidden by captivating charm.

"You have to find out about my competitors."

"I have, just preparing a summary, especially of their weaknesses."

"OK. Let me have it when I have finished resting."

"Sure, I will go for a walk and check out the competition halls."

"All right. Don't be too long." Chronis had other things on his mind as continually checking out competitor's details for Caltis. He had summarized them all. It was up to his boss now to test the water. As he turned the corner to the competition grounds, he showed his access card to the official who let him through. The halls were much the same as everywhere, perhaps the prequalifying ones a bit smaller than usual.

The single display of individual movement's competition passed, first contact fights are successful for Caltis, although he senses that he is not concentrating 100%. "You must aim for concentrating much more," Chronis comments and encourages Caltis to be motivated. Their meetings are short, commented on to the point, videos played and looked at.

In the early afternoon, Chronis meets a French-Indonesian girl standing at the food bar in the fighter's section. He notices her press card. "Are you not a pretty press officer?" He smiles at her.

"No, I am seconding my cousin and liaise with the press." She smiles back.

"May I join you?"

"Sure, but let's sit down." They exchange notes, pleasantries and talk about their respective countries.

"My name is Chronis," he offers his hand.

"I am May." She shakes his hand with a firm grip. "You must come and visit Thailand," she says.

"Well perhaps, why not. You have a warm smile." He compliments her.

"Thank you. And you have lots of charm."

"Oh now who has charm?" Her laugh captivates him.

"Are you here with a fighter?"

"Yes, with Caltis,"

"Oh - the Greek fighter."

"Yes. Are you free tonight?"

"Yes, I have a social visit late afternoon, but otherwise I am free."

"Maybe we could meet?" She looks at Chronis with querying eyes. "Here's is my cellphone number, will you let me know?"

"OK. I have to go now, my cousin has a training session and I have to present."

"What's his name?"

"Robin Amudee." Chronis remains seated and notes the name down. Perhaps she has some information that will help Caltis to have an edge over his opponents. He watches the sensual move of her hips as she stalks away. He wonders if this is her natural walk or if she just shows off. Time to join Caltis.

Chapter Seventeen
Kathy

Susan had a busy schedule of operations lately and she had relied on the help of Greg to man the security office at the clinic. The new officer she had employed had been on recommendation from the association of private body guards, Goran's friends had recommended. Greg, leader of the mercenary team, had checked on the new man and found his good reputation intact. Meanwhile Greg's men had obtained intelligence from his two men, sitting in an office close to the Martial Arts Club that Caltis' men were searching the area of Greg's safe house. He instructed his team to keep a low profile, care for Takis, but keep him in a solitary cell until further notice. His specialist interrogator had obtained some information and more would be soon forthcoming.

Susan had received hate mail, but she ignored the standard general mailbox at the Internet. Kathy checked her mail and deleted immediately all unknown senders. It was clear to her that Caltis had instructed his gang to intimidate her and smear her name. She posted a declaration to her friends and customers and reported the hate mailers to the mailbox managers. Then she identified all the doubtful senders and marked their mail as junk. This cleared Susan's public mailbox for abuse for the time being. She asked Kathy to have all telephone calls to her public phone line diverted to an answering machine, while she communicated on her private cellphone and the one for the clinic, nobody knew except the staff at the clinic and her patients and emergency cases were redirected to her private cellphone, she had changed recently. This gave her peace of mind and helped to keep her balance.

Goran, on the way to full recovery, had been transferred from Susan's secret chambers to a room within her apartment suite. With Kathy and her caring for him, he began already with basic health exercises. Anne, Goran's burn unit nurse, called Kathy to enquire about his progress.

"How is Goran?"

"He is fine, his condition is very good and he already practices basic Tai Chi."

"Fantastic. How is his face?" Anne seemed to know that he had a transplant.

"He looks gorgeous and fell in love with his new image."

"Oh, I can imagine, he is very lucky that Susan had been doing it. She is the best."

"How are you keeping Anne?"

"Very well, thank you. I am going back to England next week."

"Oh, this is a surprise. I thought you wanted to come and visit."

"Well yes, but I have to leave."

"Something the matter?" Kathy became curious.

"Well just between the two of us, I am pregnant."

"Congratulations," Kathy said surprised, thinking of Goran.

"Thank you and greetings to all. Good bye." Before Kathy could ask about the father, Anne had already replaced the receiver. But instinctively she knew. A pang of jealousy welled in her, but subsided quickly as feelings for Susan were greater. Well, she had been fond of Anne, who cared for Goran day and night with unparalleled dedication. Besides, if she had decided to have his child, it meant that she would be happy with that. Kathy mused about Goran, but she would not talk about Anne with Goran After all this is a matter between Anne and him and Anne supposed to tell him that.

Goran surfaces for breakfast, having absolved his daily morning exercises.

"And how is my favourite woman?" He kisses Kathy and hugs her.

"Thank you Goran," I feel fine and how about you?"

"I am feeling better every day. My psychic balance is restored thanks to Susan great work on my face and your love."

"I love your face." Kathy kisses his lips. She is still fond of him and her feelings have not been altogether buried with her love for Susan. "How does that feel?"

"Just great." He kisses her back.

"Gee Goran. Your kisses are just like always, perhaps even better." They kiss again. They have not noticed that Susan had entered the entrance hall and looks at their reflections in the mirror. She feels her throat tightening for a second, when she recovers. "Hi there sweethearts, I see that you are all happy and well." Goran releases Kathy and walks toward Susan. He hugs her and kisses her cheeks. Then he kisses her. "You deserve all the love form both of us." Susan kisses him back. Kathy is stirred.

She comes close to Goran hugging him from the back. Goran feels aroused with Kathy's hand on his training trunks

"Let's go all to bed," Kathy says and takes Susan and Goran's hands. From an initial gentle kissing the triad kisses all together, Goran with a deep inner sexual hunger kisses Susan, who kisses Kathy and then Goran kisses Kathy, who kisses Susan. He is carefully disrobed by Susan.

"Watch your face Goran." In the heat of a threesome, Susan watches that Goran is not stressing and asks him to stand, while she faces him. She is completely in awe of his cock stroking her belly and she and Kathy go down on him playing with her fingers, lips and tongues. Goran has felt a great urge to ejaculate but then Susan and Kathy are skillful and he experiences a great thrill of having both women seducing him at the same time.

"Relax Goran," Kathy says and her oral attentions are increasingly sensual, while Susan stands next to him and she invites his fingers to play with her pussy. "I am coming!" He cries out and jerks as he spurts into Kathy's mouth. Susan has been close to climax. She goes down to join Kathy who leaves Susan to taste Goran and she touches her from behind to enjoy Susan's climax.

Goran had to sit down on Susan's bed. His knees are shaking. He is still breathing faster, with the women sitting down next to him, on either side. Goran strokes their thighs. "How beautiful you are,' he gasps, his breathing returning to normal.

Kathy smiles and kisses Susan bending across Goran's chest. She feels his hand on her breast. Susan caresses Goran's nipple. "I love you Goran," she whispers.

"I love you Kathy," she says and they kiss.

"I love you Kathy," Goran utters and strokes her breast. "I love you Susan." His hand caresses Susan's bums, as she rose to comfort Kathy. Their caressing continuing, Kathy leaves for the bathroom. Goran is hard again. "Sit in my lap Susan. He embraces her and she rides him. Susan is hungry for sex and highly aroused. She is so excited about Goran that she climaxes. When Kathy returns, it is her turn to go to the bathroom. Kathy is excited seeing Goran's hard-on and she straddles him, to ride him. "My gorgeous Amazon," he teases her. Goran senses that Kathy is close to her climax, as he knew her sexually well, still, after such a long absence she presses hard against him, her feet circling his waist and she cries out. "Oh Goran - My man." Susan had returned and she strokes Kathy's head and kisses Goran.

They lie on Susan's wide bed. A cluster of erotic composition that had to be documented, Susan thought and she wanted to switch the video cam on with her remote. But then she saw that the red pilot light on the cam was on. Kathy! She thought immediately. All right, she had an open mind and they had documented their best love sessions before. I am glad Kathy did this. She smiled and looked at Goran, who had dozed off. His feet crossing Susan's on one side and Kathy's on the other. As she looked at Kathy, she sensed that she had similar thoughts. Kathy looked up and smiled to her. Her eyes radiated and Susan heard her saying: "It's wonderful to be in love." But it was her voice inside saying it.

Chapter Eighteen
Elena

John the Caesar had quietly slipped out Nasos' offices, where he had triggered off the self-destructive implosion that brought the upper floors down. Rushing from the scene, he disguises himself at his house, takes his gun and accessories, cash and emergency gear and departs on his old BMW motorbike. He reaches Piraeus harbour without any incident, parks his bike in the nearby parking lot belonging to a friend, locks it and walks over to the quay where the ticket offices are located. It is a clear day and albeit late autumn, the temperatures are pleasant. He buys a one way cabin ticket to Crete and walks to the 'peripteros' for a drink. There are ten minutes left to enter the boat and he is careful to stay out of sight in case the Don had employed a sniper, whose telescope would be scanning the harbour area. Between two temporary container kiosks, he samples a tin of pilsner to calm his dented nerves. Finally the boat has opened the hull and lowered the closing flap to the pier. The cars start driving into the hull of the ferry boat's dark opening that looks like a giant mouth swallowing them all. He checks out the group of tourists emerging and passing close to him, He gets up, takes his bag and mixes with the group of middle aged people. He is hardly noticed as he enters the boat and heads immediately to the escalator emerging at the first level, where the steward points him to his cabin. He locks the door, opens his bag and prepares his easy gear. He tucks his gun below his pillow and lies down. He wakes when the boat is well into the Aegean Sea. Sensing that Don's men will be after him, he has bought himself time to deal with an assassin, on his own terms now.

Elena woke from her deep sleep. She felt invigorated and yet she felt hot. Must be the wound fever, she mused. But she is sure the nurse gave her medication. She pressed the bell, but nobody responded. She got up from bed and pushed the mobile stand with an intravenous bottle on it toward the wash hand basin. The metal mirror was not perfect but she looked at a bandaged face .I am like a mummy now. She murmured and laughed. "Wow!" She gasped. "Susan must have done a real good job, but where's the nurse? These young women have other things running through their heads."

The door opened and Susan appeared. "How are you Elena?"

"I am great, a bit hot, and thirsty."

"I am sorry, but our young nurse had left suddenly."

"Oh, so soon?"

"Well there was a security breach, but it's under control now." Susan looked tired to her and she had trouble with this nurse, Maria, for sure.

"I'll organize your medication, and water. Let me check on your face." Susan was satisfied when she removed part of her bandages. "These have to be replaced right now." The summoned night nurse appeared and Susan gave her instructions to remove Elena's bandages and replaced them carefully. But she had to take her medication first, the painkillers helped Elena immediately and she went back to bed.

"In a few days you will look at a new you," the night nurse told her while she already drifted off to a welcome sleep. She floated on a silent journey to a land of tents and carpets. Welcome to magic carpet land, the dusky people greeted her. She was treated like a princess; white skinned with almond shaped eyes, the only white woman in the Sultan's kingdom. You may have a wish, the Sultan said. I want to be a racing driver. The assembled people burst into laughter, but the Sultan waved them down. If that is what my princess wishes, she shall have it. He clapped his hands and a young man appeared: Wizard, my princess wishes to become a racing driver. The wizard moved his magical wand in circles and triangles, up and down and around. With a swooshing sound she stood in full racing gear next to a red Audi R8 sports car, her best and trusted high performance vehicle. The race was on, she had to warm up and this time after a flying start she was placed in second position. It turned out to be spectacular and a tough scramble began for best places before the next bend. She was third, but soon she passed the Nissan sports car in front of her.

Down the long straight to the grandstand she clocked best time and her team jumped up and down: *Monroe of racing*, the banners read. Her adrenalin started choking her as she passed the Daihatsu in front of her. Hold steady now, she heard the voice from her racing stable in her headphones and she could hardly answer. Then she heard "Go for it now.' and she put her foot down.

"You've won, you've won! The voice over her headphones started shrieking. She slowed down not even realizing that she had passed the checquered flag and headed for the first bend. Her car held out well and she patted the steering wheel. Waving to the crowd, she slowed down to stop at her stable. Her mechanics lifted her up and moved her on their shoulders to the winner's podium. There she stood high above her opponents, the only woman who had made this race in the last years, besides won it in convincing style. She received the silver beaker and a bottle of Moet and Chandon. She sprayed the champagne over the heads of the other two winners who doused her face with champagne. It felt good, almost sexual. You look great baby, they lauded her. She shook the bottle, as she had seen so many times on TV, and sprayed the rest of the champagne on top of her fans, taking sips in between.

In her stable she was celebrated and the party was in full swing. Suddenly a man appeared with a dark and sinister look, somebody she had seen before, He approached her. "You have abused us and made money on us, an accessory for the killing of a racing colleague, you have to die." He pointed a gun at her…

Elena woke and her body perspired. She sat up and loosened the ties of her blue gown and pulled it up over her stomach. She still had a good figure. But this alp had unsettled her. She touched herself. It felt good. Then she climaxed she moved up again pulled her gown down and went back to bed. She had avoided to become emotionally charged, but this dream had made her aroused, as every time she raced a car she enjoyed a great climax afterwards.

John the Caesar had slept well. In the morning he woke early and checked the position of the boat. It would anchor at Heraklion within two hours' time. He slipped into his overcoat, donned his hat and lit his pipe. A small walk would be great to loosen the limbs. He walked up the stairs and exited the boat on the second floor. As he turned the corner to the front deck he felt a stabbing pain on his head and collapsed. "It's him," a voice said and tossed his hat into the sea below.

"How do you know?" The man pulled John's false moustache off.

"You are right the chubby fellow said and kicked John's rib. He aimed his gun fitted with a silencer and shot him into his temple. The other guy took a few photographs. "Now we have proof he is dead and we earned the bounty on his head." They lifted him up and threw him overboard. Nobody had noticed the incident. The two men disappeared into the other direction.

Chapter Nineteen
Chronis

Caltis has lost his spirit, his inner tai chi and he gives way to dark thoughts. While he misses to train harder and longer hours, he is drifting off to a Paris nightclub. Chrysos has warned him, but he has no strength himself, to influence Caltis to train harder. Instead he hangs out with May, whose cousin had lost the quarterfinals.

"Robin is mad at me," May says to Chronis, as they meet for their tete-a-tete.

"Why is that?"

"He complains that I have not given him the correct dose of Coca tea, he has been used to drink. Nobody ever complained as the substance was similar to drinking strong coffee or green tea. However, I did not use the triple dose."

"You could let me try some, I am not fighting." He laughed.

"Sure I can get you some." May said and opened the buttons of his shirt. He kissed her and his fingers played with her child-like breasts. She started arousing him. May had a knack for giving Chronis pleasure and asked him about lovemaking styles. They bantered and played.

"You have to use a condom," May insisted.

"Nah," Chronis sighed, "I dislike condoms.

"OK," May said, 'Let's do it the Greek way then." He laughed.

Later May left to retrieve some of the coca tea. Chronis was still asleep as she returned. May prepared the tea, placed some cookies she had brought along, into a jar and tried the tea. It tasted just fine. Chronis stirred. "May is that you?"

"Yes love, I am back."

"Oh you've made tea." He stretched, got up, slipped into his sports outfit and joined her. He took a sip. "Mh, it tastes just like a strong green tea."

"Yes, but the effect is greater."

"Aha, I am curious."

"Well, it takes at least half an hour or more to take effect."

"I guess it depends on one's metabolism."

"Yes." May stood up and poured herself more tea."

"Leave some leaves for tonight."

"What have you planned for the evening?"

"Maybe a romantic evening on a Bateau Mouche?"

"That would be super." She kissed him.

Caltis returned from his training session and looked tired. The colour had drained from his cheeks and he had constantly a desire to lie down. Chronis knocked at his door and entered.

"Hi Chronis, what's up?"

"I brought you some rejuvenating tea."

"Cut the crap, what's that?"

"It's coca tea."

"Well if it's of help and not a traceable stimulant, it'll be a hit." He sipped the cup offered to him. "Mh, first impression - taste is great." Chronis smiled.

"I leave you another dose for another cup here, just place the leaves into a cup and pour hot water over it." Caltis felt tired and went to lie down again. As Chronis started to leave, he fell into deep slumber.

"The Bateau Mouche boat trip proved to be a great romantic stimulant to Chronis and May. Perhaps it had been also due to the coca tea. Chronis felt great and the dinner was to their liking. The lights along the route were just perfect highlighting the trip with famous city landmarks lit up. "It feels like birthday, May said and her feet played up on Chronis' legs. She fell more and more in love with him. He had opened to her a complete new perspective to making love.

She was listening with her whole being to Chronis, who wooed her with endearments, caressing her feet back under the table and he sank completely into the magical almond ponds of her eyes. The evening had the atmosphere that meant to her being in Paris. A clear evening with lights playing a glittering game on the river Seine, from the lit up monuments they passed by. She became increasingly tipsy and it might have been the coca tea, she had before. I think I am sinking into the river of love, she whispered to Chronis who kissed her hand. He was a good lover, May thought about their lovemaking, looking into the night, as if she would see a video tape with their embraces locked together. She often wondered how their lovemaking would appear to her if depicted on a video clip.

"A penny for your thoughts, Chronis said.

"I saw us together....:" she said gazing through the glazed canopy...

"Where?"

"In my mind."

"Aha, like a video clip?"

Yes." She smiled.

"I did not know..."

"Well it was just an idea..." she cut in.

"Can be arranged," he replied, "next time I let the video cam run." He raised his glass to hers and they toasted.

"The Eiffel Tower," the accompanying commentary sounded from a tour operator.

"I love it," May said. Chronis nodded and sampled desert.

Caltis felt magically awake and his energies were restored to a great extent. He felt restless. He had rested well, the night was young and his next fight was only after lunch tomorrow. He had time for himself. A red pamphlet lay on the side table next to the entrance. He took it to the easy chair, sat down and then looked at it: *Crazy Horse Saloon.* It read in bold writing. He had heard about it. Now there was a chance to have a look at it. He phoned reception to book a place for him at the bar counter.

At first he felt uneasy of bending his rules of adhering to sleep, training and proper nourishment during competitive fighting. But once the lights dimmed and music filled the room, the stage became the focal point of his attention. A woman appeared, then another. They danced around a horizontal pole as a third woman appeared. Light projections enhanced the colourful scene and geometrical patterns changed, greatly enhancing the slender bodies of the dancers. The scenes changed in succession with the music and Caltis, lost in thought, drifted on a cloud, far away from fighting and from ambitions of becoming a king in the world of martial arts clubs and *kungfu* fighting styles.

The show lasted an hour and Takis was most taken and stirred by the dancer with one leg in a high nylon stocking. He finished his drink and left the club ahead of the crowds. He had not noticed that the club was packed to capacity, until he had to squeeze past the masses to the exit. The fresh night air revived him. A woman accosted him and as he did not say a word while she carried on, hooking her arm into his and he accompanied her into the nearby hotel. She whispered her price into his ear. He nodded.

She dropped her clothes. "Just one stocking," he said and she obliged, "ah," she gasped, "just like at the club?"

"Oh, you know?"

"Yes, I used to be a dancer there." She moved her well-kept body and danced for him, getting closer and opening his waist button.

"Just give me head," he uttered, "I have to be up early." She smiled.

"You have well developed muscles. Sportsman?"

"Yes, kungfu fighter."

"AH, what have we here, a little kungfu fighter?" She teased his growing erection and asked him to lie back. "You are too tense! Let me relax you." Caltis had never experienced such a skillful fellatio.

"Let go," she said after a while breathing in and continuing her oral act. Initial strange feelings due to his tensed up body soon converted to good feelings that changed rapidly into fire that started at the pit of his stomach and spread up his torso. He burst into flames that seemed to consume his whole body in a flash.

"AH!" he gasped out in succession and could not control his breathing as he was used to.

"Gee," you are something else."

"Good?"

"Indeed." He lay on the bed and she joined him lighting a cigarette. "You don't mind?"

"No."

"Let me look at your body. I want to see all of it." She stroked his chest and neck, touched every muscle and turned him around stroking his buttocks. When she caressed his perineum, he became hard again. "Damned!" he swore into his breath. She turned him and smiled.

"Ah the little kungfu fighter is up again for action. He could not protest as she straddled him and moved sensually on him. "Like an Amazon," he thought, touching her small breasts with their pointed nipples. Then he recalled his training session in the morning. He grabbed her waist and rolled her aside. "But Monsieur I am not finished yet."

"Never mind come back tomorrow."

"Oh, you have to fight?"

"Yes I have an intensive training session tomorrow late morning."

"She straddled him again. But this will relax you. You can sleep here." Caltis felt in heaven and slept like a baby. He stirred and got up. She was gone. He took the card from the spot on the side table where he had placed the money. It read *Madeleine, your personal dancer.* A telephone number scribbled on.

Caltis cleaned up, rushed from the dingy hotel, crossed over to the other side of the road and waved a taxi down. Arriving at the competition grounds, he paid the cabbie and walked light-footed to have breakfast at the competitor's mess hall. It had just opened and he did not expect seeing Chronis, who had a probably a night out with his Thai girlfriend. When he looked for his cellphone in his pocket, he came across Madeleine's card. He thought of her lovemaking skills and felt an inner stirring. Had the coca tea that Chronis gave him yesterday have an additional effect on his libido?

Chapter Twenty
Kathy & Susan

Kathy has never felt better in her entire life. She had prepared lunch for Goran and Susan. Since they had their first erotic encounter together, the triad has agreed to a ménage-a-trois. It happened intuitively and she wondered if Susan's part had not been in lieu of compensation she desired for her strenuous work at her clinic. Joachim, her partner had taken in more responsibility and they shared the work and the benefits of income. Besides he was always pleasant and kept his personal life private. Susan never interfered, but she felt that at one stage, when she had a crush on him, he acted reserved and withdrawn. Perhaps he is into gender love, she thought and as such I am too. She still felt sexually more drawn to Kathy than to Goran, even if they had sex together.

Kathy felt that she had a split personality in sexual matters, as she loved Susan intensely, but on other occasions she preferred Goran's lovemaking. In a discussion with Susan, who became increasingly jealous of her, making passionate love to Goran, she had blurted out: Susan I love you very much and want you, but I miss with you the act of penetration. Susan said nothing and Kathy embraced her. She realized that Susan loved her more. However between the three of them, tensions were seldom elongated to turn into problems, as one of them, usually Goran had the ability and sensible attitude to smooth emotional matters over with a kiss, a touch, some kind words and endearments. For her he remained the most wonderful person she had ever met and ideal partner to share with Susan, who never placed any demands on him, except on her.

Goran had taken up his Tai Chi training sessions with Greg, the mercenary, who became an ideal partner to bring out in Goran his talent for a quick succession of stances, which he worked on him to complement Goran's excellent had-pushing techniques. Slowly Goran has gained speed and Greg estimated that he was already up to 70 percent of his capacity. They trained in one of Susan's secret rooms, with a special security attached and a small office annexed, where Greg had his laptop installed for continual contact with his security gang, who observed Caltis' home, his social connections and the Martial Arts Club.

"Come on Goran let's have another round."

"All right, after that we have a break."

"I have to leave anyway. Now let's see your stances in succession." Goran started with all basic stances but he combined them in quick successions as his partner attacked him with increasing speed. Goran twisted Greg and turned him downed to the floor. Greg got up. "Well done Goran, you are becoming fighting fit again."

"Thanks for partnering me Greg." He stretched out his hand and Greg took it. Then he made a surprise turn to throw Goran, who retaliated.

"Aha, you have instinctive reactions working." Greg left for the shower and changed into his casual gear, slipping into the holster for his gun. They sat down and Goran fetched cold drinks.

"Your two women are doing wonders for you my friend!" Goran smiled.

"I see that your girlfriend has arrived with the Mitsubishi," Goran pointed to the surveillance cam at the entrance downstairs.

"Oh - Jo? She is a darling, secretary and love interest." He smiled. "I have checked her out. She is clean and under observation as all of us, constantly."

"OK, let's be ready for the time Caltis returns from the championship fights."

"We will be. You know Goran we are on stand-by." He packed his laptop into his bag, checked his watch and left Goran behind.

Kathy had watched the news followed by sports news. She prepared the table. The voice of the newsreader startled her. "Racing news: The latest results from the European Champion-ships in sports car racing. Symin, a young talented woman has come up in sports car racing. She is leading the points." Kathy saw Elena's new face depicted on the screen. She recognized her immediately. She had dyed her hair to brunette and her facial features were leaner with her almond shaped eyes. She looked oriental. Susan and Joachim did a fantastic job on her. She would not be recognized as Elena again. Kathy was glad that she had done a deal with Susan and escaped the clutches of Takis and the underground. She would make a name for herself in Germany and Kathy was sure she would clinch the championship. Elena - Symin - would be poised to become an icon in motorsport.

Goran enters Susan's apartment. "Hi Goran," Kathy rushes to give him a kiss. "You look great, have you worked out?" Goran hugs Kathy, kissing her back.

"Yes, I had a good training session with Greg. What's up?"

"I have prepared lunch."

"Mh, smells great."

"It's steak veggies and dumplings in a mustard sauce."

"Ah, you cooked one of my favourite foods." Goran beams. He circles her waist as she serves the starters and kisses her.

There's a click on the door lock and Susan enters. "Ah, my two sweethearts! Let me hug you." She kisses Kathy and then Goran.

"It smells great. Kathy you are spoiling us."

"It's my pleasure. Sit down and let's enjoy the starters."

"This crab cocktail is delicious Kathy." Goran has opened the chardonnay and filled their glasses. "A toast to us! "They clink their glasses.

"Goran you look well today," Susan lauds his looks. She is proud of creating him successfully a new face.

"This is my gratitude to you Susan that you have, besides giving me a new life, helped me return to it fully. " He takes Susan's hand and kisses it. Then he continues: Thanks to your masterly skills that rendered me a face that is every man's envy and for your love sharing it with Kathy and me. It has sped up my inner healing process and killed most of my deep hate against my enemies."

Susan is stirred and her heart goes out for Goran for the first time with a deeper feeling, she is astounded to have found again for a man. She glows and Kathy feels a flash of jealousy. She smiles und raises her glass: "To us!"

"To us," Kathy replies and Goran takes Kathy's hand and kisses it, before he raises his glass.

The meal has been well received and Kathy had served a fruit flan for desert. Goran has a phone call from Greg, who had received a tape about Caltis, he wants him to see. Goran leaves after tasting his desert

Kathy and Susan sit together sipping coffee and Kathy thinks about their future together. How long will their ménage-a-trois last?

"A penny for your thoughts!" Susan says.

"Susan, I wanted to discuss with you our investment portfolio."

"Oh yes. We have a substantial shareholding in the Martial Arts Clubs."

"Well it's our money we won on Elena and the shares Goran wrote over to us."

"I kept the investments separated."

"Oh that's great."

"My broker's advice."

"I thought…" Kathy stops.

"Tell me."

"Well we could help Goran to get onto his feet again. "

"Yes, of course."

"He deserves ownership of the club again."

"Well Kathy, this task is at present in discussion from Greg's side."

"Oh Susan I am so afraid something might happen to us." Susan has never experienced Kathy like this, riddled with emotion and fear. Kathy needs her love, she thinks and she hugs her friend and soulmate.

"Come Kathy, all will come right, even if it seems difficult at present." She kisses her and the sweethearts caress each other.

"Come with me Kathy." She takes Kathy by her hand and whispers "One good sensual culinary time deserves another sensual time. Kathy follows her to the bedroom.

Chapter Twenty One
Chronis

Caltis has missed many opportunities to train with good Tai Chi fighters and he has been convinced by Chronis that May's cousin Robin would be great to train with before the semifinals tomorrow.

"You need to sharpen up," he utters to Caltis, after the night he had spent with May, while Caltis has stayed out all night.

"Training, training, dear Caltis and no loose women!" He scolds his employer. Caltis looks at him with anger welling up in him.

"See, who is talking!" He yells at Chronis. "You smart ass, screwing every night your Thai bitch!" Chronis reacts annoyed.

"You have chosen company with bad language. I resent you calling May a bitch!"

"And you better watch your obligations and organize my training sessions. Have you forgotten about that?" Chronis feels bad. He had neglected Caltis, preferring the company of May and her cousin.

"I am sorry; I will make it up to you."

"How"? Tomorrow is a most important fight. The most important one in my career. I have never thought to come this far. Your input had been minimal. Any ideas?"

"I have organized a few training sessions with Robin, starting in half an hour's time." Caltis looked out the window, as if searching for inspiration. He saw Madeleine's head and back as she kneeled before him...he smelled her scent of rose perfume...

"Ok I will be ready. But let's discuss strategy after my session."

"All right I will arrange it." Chronis said and departed.

When Chronis arrived at the training hall, Robin was already warming up, practicing stances. He waved at him as he paused.

"Caltis, will be coming just now."

"All right."

"He needs sharpening up," Chronis said and raised his eyebrows. He still felt the night out with May that ended with passionate lovemaking. His senses were constantly inundated with visions of May's erotic movements on him and her expressive passion. He had to constantly concentrate on his tasks ahead to help Caltis to reach his goal and win the finals. As he saw May handing him coca tea, he snapped his fingers, calling him back from his vision. That's it! He made a few steps of Sirtaki and smiled feeling lightheaded.

"You seem to be in elated spirits," May came closer and kissed him. He kissed her back

"Yes, you and I yesterday - just so wonderful…pleasures of love." He made another few dance steps. "What are you dancing?"

"Sirtaki."

"Aha, like in Zorba the Greek."

"Ah you know."

"Everybody knows the movie." Caltis arrived and Chronis introduced him to May and then to Robin. He shook hands, murmured a few words and stepped onto the mat. The fighters warmed up and showed off their Tai Chi movements to each other. Then they started with first basic hand pushing and Robin showed Caltis some new moves, he had watched on a video. "These are movements your next opponent will have in store." I know because I have trained with him too." Caltis was impressed.

Chronis talked to May about a dream he had. He told her about having slipped some drops of a tranquilizer into the energy drink of an opponent he had to fight. A beautiful woman who appeared like a nymph from a fairy tale handed him a drink that immediately revived him and he could beat his opponent with newfound energy.

"Sounds like an interesting idea." May said, "I should have tried that for my cousin's fight and he would have won by points, not by losing one." Chronis raised his eyebrows. "Mh. You think it could be done?" May looked down.

"Let's choose a quiet corner." She went ahead and Chronis followed. At the end of the hall they found a cubicle reserved for the press.

"I have a friend who is related to the trainer."

"You don't say" Chronis bowed his head close to May's and she whispered.

"Usually half an hour before his warm up, he sips an energy drink."

"But how can you persuade your friend to spike his drink?"

"She hates her uncle's guts, as he molested her once."

"Aha that explains it."

"She could do it when the training session is over tonight."

"Aha. What the heck! This is a golden opportunity." He looked at her.

"It will cost a bit of bribing money though." Chronis had thought about it. Caltis still had some cash available for expenses.

"How much?" Olivia saw her opportunity.

"5000." The sum seemed reasonable to Chronis.

"OK, I will discuss it with Caltis and let you know after his training session is over." May looked at him questioningly and Chronis caught on.

"There is still the coca, if you need some for Caltis."

"Yes of course, I need a double portion."

"That is for another 2000." Chronis nodded. May stood up and he followed her lost in thought. Even if the drops did not slow down Caltis' opponent, the coca would revive him and give him a greater edge. He smiled.

"What are you smiling about?" Caltis' voice startled him. "I have good news for you," Caltis said. "So have I," Chronis replied, 'but have a shower first."

Chronis told Caltis that with the help of his girlfriend, they could lower the reaction of his opponent and give Caltis the greater edge for the fight. Caltis smiled, he began to like his aide and comrade-in-arms. "You better make it work!" he said to Chronis, agreeing to the bribe money and he went to rest. Chronis agreed to meet May at the Café Deux Magots in the Latin Quarter. It usually teemed with tourists.

The cab took Chronis to the Latin Quarter. He asked the driver to stop at a corner close to the café. He paid and stepped into a niche nearby where he remained for a few minutes, just to make sure nobody followed him. Then he rushed to meet May.

He saw her at the back far from the entrance. It smelled of fresh ground coffee and anise seed.

"Hi May." he kissed her.

"Do you have the money?"

"Yes." He handed her the envelope.

"Great! "

"Please May make it stick!"

"Yes I will." she answered and stuck the envelope into the inside pocket of her jacket. The waiter appeared and Chronis ordered a small beer, while May asked for green tea. "Ah," she said, "your coca." She handed him a packet, which he placed into his pocket. "Thanks May."

"Thanks Chronis. It's nice doing business with you."

"The same here." He smiled. "And now let's do what all sweethearts do in Paris." He kissed her.

She had taken a cab back to the sports compound, where she had arranged to meet her friend Olivia, who rushed fleet footed at the agreed meeting point. No use of cellphones, Chronis has ordered, so communication could not be traced. Just in case. They walked the grounds toward the facilities. In the change room cubicle she handed Olivia the drop extract she had been given by a Bolivian herbalist in a Thai run shop when Robin had severe pain and could not sleep. It had a tranquilizing effect.

She had filled some into a small vial, she handed Olivia together with 1000 up-front payment
of the 2000, promised to her.
"You get the other 1000 when the job had been
done satisfactory."
"OK, I won't let you down."
"Swear!" Olivia raised her hand.
The remainder of the cash handed over to her
by Chronis was meant for her risk and all expenses, besides she had to care for investments for her family's pension. But she wouldn't
tell anybody. "Listen Olivia, do it carefully and
wipe the bottle. There must be no fingerprints."
"OK." She hugged her. Olivia liked her, she
could sense that. She kissed her and Olivia left
her soulmate to be well ahead of her, as agreed.

Chapter Twenty Two
May

Olivia has cleaned the change room of her uncle. She locks the door and prepares the vial,
May gave her. She opens the fridge and takes
the green bottle with the prepared energy drink.
She has watched her uncle's trainer before
placing it. Unscrewing the cap she carefully
puts six drops, as instructed, into the drink, replaces the cap, swaying it. Then she puts her

gloves on and cleans the bottle from her fingerprints, replaces it at the same place and wipes
the fridge door and handle. She pockets the vial
and the gloves, unlocks the door, peeking outside and with nobody is in sight, she exits, clos-
es the door and locks it. Then she walks with
her usual gait to her room at the staff quarters.
She takes a shower, dons her bathrobe, sets
the alarm on her cellphone and reclines on her
bed.

May had retired writing her journal, keeping up
a family tradition, as her father had encouraged
her, himself a great journal writer. She took the
routine up seriously after he had died in a traffic
accident, a year ago. Since then she had been
taken care of by the family of her first cousin,
where she has helped with household chores,
until Robin has employed her as his personal
assistant. She worked her way up to this trust-
worthy position, acting at first as a messenger
for confidential information. In time Robin would
entrust her with research on all she could find
about Tai Chi fighting. Besides she had started
a data base for all Tai Chi fighters, trainers and
schools, first locally, then extending her files to
China, Europe and the international scene. Tai
Chi fighting had been made popular with movies, called in America *kungfu.* However her re-

search expanded to the field of nutrition and herbal medicines. She found Thai shops worldwide and contacted the shop in Paris, where she sourced her coca tea leaves and other ingredients mixed by a talented Thai woman, who had travelled South America and studied plants and herbs for years, using the imports in her shop. Her family had always been related to Thai kickboxing sports and some family members had excelled in it in the past. Robin had been to China on a study tour demonstrating Thai boxing. He made some friends who introduced him to Tai Chi fighting. He passed his basic training with flying colours and started to train other fighters in Thailand. His efforts of organizing an exchange of training facilities and tournaments in China and Thailand paid off through the years and some top fighters emerged also in Thailand. He was one of them qualifying for the European Masters Championships.

May had been in good luck to meet Chronis, who befriended her. She valued his friendship being the personal assistant and aide to Caltis, a talented fighter from Greece, who had a specific talent in throwing his opponents. As soon as her cousin Robin had been beaten in the quarterfinals by a ferocious fighter from England, she sensed an opportunity to assist Chronis, who searched for all the help he could get to support his employer to win these championships. She sensed she could make an additional income from consulting Chronis on herbal medicines and supplements, but she received supplies too late for Robin's fight. Her Thai source in Paris had advised her in uses of coca and yerba mate for stimulating muscle suppleness and tenacity, while she also learned about mixtures and tinctures slowing reactions down.

She had tried out some of them on Chronis and on herself and Chronis had given Caltis some coca tea to drink. It worked well for being stimulated with extra energies for her and her friend for a romantic evening that ended with passionate lovemaking. She was convinced, as she had been informed that it also created energy for a sportsman to endure in hard competitive fights. The first batch of coca leaves had helped Caltis to win his semifinal fight and secure himself a place in the finals. She got up, dressed, pocketed the coca leaves and headed for the taxi ranks.

Olivia woke and dressed, took her bag and walked to the competition hall. She had to witness the fight. She had done what May had asked her and would enjoy seeing her uncle lose the fight. She had been assured that nobody would even suspect a thing. The herbal mixture was safe and undetectable in the bloodstream for a doping test.

The competitors had warmed up, exhibited their individual movements to the jurors and were poised to start the competition. Caltis felt great, but something bothered him. His opponent, an Armenian of Turkish extraction, had demonstrated some stances he was not familiar with. Neither Chronis, nor May had mentioned that to him, although they had done background research on him.

The fight started and for the first contacts the Armenian had the upper hand. Caltis regained some points on hand-pushing fights and yet the Armenian was ahead. As the fight continued, Caltis noticed that his opponent lost some of his fighting edge, but perhaps he himself became more alert and gained on sharpness, while the other waned. Caltis changed tactics and varied his stances accordingly in quicker successions as usual and attacked the burly fighter for a throw. The Greek fans cheered him as he succeeded and although the Armenian hung on, Caltis could shake him visibly more and more as the fight continued. Gaining confidence he succeeded to equalize the points and then move ahead on scoring. The Greek quarter supported him with encouraging calls. Chronis could hardly retain his joy, but he stayed cool. Caltis, who had started off in an indifferent mood, appearing intimidated, gained increasingly confidence and Chronis noticed his energy burst with a second throw of his opponent. From then on there was no holding back for Caltis, on the way of winning his semifinal bout. With the final throw he boosted his points and remembered to show his aesthetical form to complete his winning in style. He emphasized his otherwise economical movements with beautiful circles of arm swings interspersed by the geometry of leg kicks and stances, classical standards of Tai Chi, which pleased the jurors. The fight ended with the Armenian dropping his shoulders in the woes of defeat. They remained in a resting stance for a few seconds, bowed with respect to the jurors and then walked to their teams. Caltis had been awarded top spot and his team and fans jubilated.

Chronis embraced Caltis. "Slow down now," he whispered into his ear. Caltis felt still charged up and Chronis tried hard to calm him down.

"I could have smashed the guy for good," Caltis mumbled and Chronis asked his team members to assist him accompanying Caltis to his quarters. He was hot from a fever and he mumbled continually. It was clear to Chronis that the dosage of coca had a great effect on him, even within the limits that were not suspicious in his fighting behaviour and not detectable, if queried by the opponent's team for a doping test. Besides Caltis did not commit irregularities and the time for a protest had soon collapsed anyway. The jurors had given him green light and by now he was officially accepted as a fighter in the finals.

The Armenian team could not believe that their top fighter had lost. The man claimed that he had a day off and left it at that. But his trainer became suspicious and fed him rumours of irregularities. Yet the team manager had accepted the defeat of his best fighter, seconded by the team doctor, who could not find anything wrong with him. The team had to pack it in and swallow the bitter pill of defeat, which had become a sombre scene of swallowing root beers and meeting for a moratorium at their change rooms.

Olivia had left her seat at the back row, as soon as Caltis had been declared the winner. She avoided some of the team members and excused herself to have an early night. Inside she jubilated, as she had the other half of the payment now due to her. She would meet May later tonight at the toilets of the local eatery that had a coffee house attached. She lay down on her

bed, switched her cellphone to music and relaxed.

Caltis lay on the massage table of his change
room, with Chronis present, who observed the
masseur. When Caltis had relaxed, taken a
shower and dressed, he accompanied him with
another team member to his quarters. He lied
down on his bed and snoozed off. Chronis noticed that the fight had not exhausted him, but
as soon as the coca effect waned, he became
tired and disinterested even in the final fight
result and his trusted friend May might be still
able to provide coca leaves for him, but she had
no connection to the camp of their opponent in
the finals.
Caltis' condition was definitely a psychic problem and Chronis had no access to Caltis' cellphone, as he had a habit of locking it up in his
drawer. He must have received bad news, Caltis mused. He accessed his laptop and tried
connecting first to Alex, but he was offline. The
agreed website, CATA, of Caltis' personal gang
had not been updated. "Damned Castor," he
murmured, "he had not kept his promise to report instantly to him about the stand of matters
at the club." Something was wrong, Chronis
had a bad gut feel. But he had to avoid asking

Caltis about it, as he intended to rather be jovial and render a good psyche for Caltis' final bout.

He would meet May early morning tomorrow and obtain the coca and bring her the requested payment. He definitely needed more coca for the final fight preparations, starting with a spiked late breakfast and ask May about dosages she thought necessary to get Caltis into ship-shape, as she had witnessed his fighting today. However, he had agreed with her beforehand that he would need more supplies if Caltis would win the fight today.

Chapter Twenty Three
Kathy, Susan & Goran

Susan had fixed breakfast while Goran and Kathy still slept. Goran appeared first
"Good morning Susan."
"Good morning Goran." He kissed her.
"Have you slept well?"
"Yes, thanks to you girls I am a reborn and happy man." Since Goran received his new face, he felt different, on the trails of another life that held great promises and a new agenda of priorities he had set for himself to conquer back what rightfully belonged to him. He would unmask the corrupt board at the Martial Arts Club

and confront the murderous gang of Caltis, then deal with the criminal leader himself. He had forgiven Elena, who gave him her blood and saved his life. He was glad that she confessed to Susan and Cathy and highlighted the events of the plot that brought about his accident. Iannis, Kathy's boyfriend had been executed by the mob, but for Elena it would have meant the same fate. Susan had proposed a way out with her generosity and open mind and Elena looked up to her. Susan sensed Gordon's thought around his new appearance. It is perfectly normal that he has to find a new way of dealing with that, she thought and fetched a can of tea, she had prepared.

"You are deep into thinking, Goran."

"I had to run through my priorities, as I do every morning." He looked serious.

"I am sure you will just do fine and catch up to your old life."

"I think I have a new life and a new agenda, but old scores to settle."

"You are healed Goran, but do not forget to take your medication regularly."

"Thanks Susan, I will, doc." He smiled. He had never addressed me doc before, Susan liked his spirit that indicated to her that his psyche was uplifted and soon Goran would tackle the dark and sinister world. She was sure that he

162

came out of this most important battle of his life as a winner. Susan poured Green tea for Goran and then for herself. Kathy came into the room.

"Good morning my two most important persons in my life, soulmates and lovers, best friends and family." She hugged Goran and kissed him, then she hugged Susan who brought new toast and jam.

"Hi Kathy, you had a long sleep today."

"Yes, I felt like lying in a bit longer, dreaming of you."

"Tell us Kathy," Goran said.

"Well we celebrated our union with a picnic. Driving to the Parnassos mountain range, we joined a procession to Delphi. We had been magically transported back into Antiquity, with white flowing peplos garbs in Ionian style. At the sanctuary we paid our fees for having our future told by Pythia, sitting on a tripod, vapour streaming from a cleft in the rock below her. I felt dizzy…"

"So what did she prophesize you?" Susan became curious.

"I have to recall it, wait. Yes, she said: You will take an unusual path that arrives at a two way junction. Taking the left one will bring you back to it and taking the right means eternal life…"

"It's a strange dream," Goran said, while Susan remained silent with a serious facial expression.

Then he continued, "however, an interesting dream needing some interpretations." He started to tease her and they laughed. Susan stood up. "I will get you soft boiled eggs."

"What is our program today Susan?"

"I thought of going shopping to the new mall in town."

"Excellent, I would need a new casual outfit." Kathy said.

"They have every type of shop there and also an excellent coffee shop."

"Goran you will watch over us, will you?" Kathy beamed. He looked sexy this morning with his tussled golden hair, just like a young Achilles, she mused. Yet Goran had developed a special habit, observing his face wherever he had an opportunity and if he passed a window reflecting his image. He had become self-conscious of his new image and a hang to a narcissistic trend, Kathy mused. Mentioning this to Susan, who replied that this had been expected, and Susan pointed out to her the psychological process, besides she assured Kathy that in time his self-admiration of his new face would disappear, as he became used to his new looks and identified himself with it. Kathy though was not that sure, she knew Goran better than Susan and felt a deeper bond with him.

"...Yes..., of course." replied Goran, who was lost in thought. Kathy bent over to him and kissed him. Goran thought immediately about contacting Greg, as agreed, whenever they had to leave the protection of their monitored suites. He apologized and murmured he had to get ready and left to his room. Opening his laptop he established immediate communication with Greg. On the secure private website he started messaging him. Greg responded and would act as agreed to their protocol.

Goran drove Susan's BMW 4x4, he enjoyed driving, He took the main motorway to the new shopping complexes and started with 'Athens Heart', he choose to see if they were followed. With Greg at a reasonable distance, Goran could not see anybody closer interested in them. The girls could not find a shop carrying the type of clothes Kathy wanted. After a short stop for a drink, where Goran conversed shortly with Greg using SMS communication, to inform him of their next movements, he drove to Kifissia Avenue, where two big shopping malls had been opened a few years back. Susan thought of trying the 'Golden Hall' first. There would be another shopping complex on the same busy avenue further on, if they could not find a casual outfit for Kathy, while Susan needed some specific stationary and a pair of suede sneakers for her jean outfit, which Kathy thought suited her so well.

Goran parked at the centre and walked behind the two women that had shaped his life and he would protect them with his own if necessary. But with Greg around they were watched like best of VIP's. However the devil never sleeps, he mused and checked Greg's position. He became extremely alert since the verbal and written threats thrown at Susan, which she ignored and let him and Greg handle and find their sources. Greg had placed his men on high alert in case of an emergency.

Susan purchased her stationary and followed Kathy to a boutique, which had outfits of Kathy's taste. Goran watched the entrance to the shop and signaled to Greg their position. Greg had followed them in a safe distance, with his driver, while his men followed him with another car. Once Kathy had selected her lilac outfit, Susan commented on the unusual colour that suited to Kathy's black hair and brown eyes. "Just great! It fits you perfectly," she said and smiled. Kathy felt happy and Susan asked her to wear her outfit right away. Kathy asked the sales assistant to pack her other clothes and she paid with her credit card. Then she followed Susan to a shoe shop on the ground floor. Susan found a pair to her liking and she was in good luck as the pair fitted her like a glove.

"Just leave them on Susan," Kathy beamed, "let's enjoy our new purchases."

"Indeed," Susan replied. "Let's have something to eat."

"All right." They called Goran and passed a shop for men's clothes. Kathy looked at Susan. "Come with me." She pulled Susan into the shop. "I saw a cute thin jersey in a blue colour, just great for Goran." She bought it and asked for it to be packed as a present. "Don't tell Goran, it's for his birthday."

"All right Kathy, it's so attentive of you." Kathy smiled and Susan looked at her soulmate. Kathy was a darling and always keen to bring joy to her friends around her. Besides she meant the world to Susan. She took her arm and they entered a coffee shop that Susan had read about, having first class homemade scones.

Goran could not relax and he wished to have this shopping outing behind him. Something bothered him, but he could not put his finger to it. Even the thought of Greg's presence nearby could not pacify his strange feelings. But Kathy's good mood and Susan's banter took his mind off for some moments.

"I think we should move shortly," Goran said in a low voice, stood up and moved to pay the bill.

"It's my invitation," Susan said and asked the passing lass for the bill. Goran ushered the girls outside and checked for anything unusual, but he saw nothing that alerted him. As they moved to from the lift to the parking level, Goran saw the flicker of a reflection of light. The sound of dull thud from a silencer gun followed at the same time. Goran shouted to duck as Kathy turned in front of Susan and with one jump pulled the two women down to the floor. A second thudding sound came from the lift wall. Gordon raised his gun and fired in the direction of the assassin. He activated his cellphone and shouted for help. Greg rushed to the garage and alerted his men, who shot at a dark clothed man with a balaclava on his head. He fell wounded and Greg's men jumped to arrest him. Goran shouted "Kathy!" She lay still and a pool of blood soaked her new outfit. Goran tore his shirt off and tried to stop the bleeding. "AMBU-LANCE!" He shouted, but Greg who rushed to the spot had already called for one.

"Kathy, Kathy!" Susan cried and joined her in the ambulance, where first aid was immediately applied to Kathy.

Goran sat on the floor next to the pool of blood and Greg helped him up. "Come on Goran let's get to the clinic." He spoke to his men who had treated the assassin and removed a bullet. He was locked into their medical room and observed. "In no way must he be handed to the police," Greg ordered.

"He's in the safe house," one of his men replied. "Watch him and call me when he opens his eyes." Greg took the parcels from the shopping and locked them into Susan's car and drove Goran to the clinic. His comrade followed him with Greg's car.

Goran's thoughts circled around the assassination. It must have been Susan they were after, but Kathy took the bullet. "Damned bastards!" Goran shouted and hit his fist onto the dashboard.

"OK Goran try to relax, we caught the guy,"

"I want to see him!" Goran shouted.

"I will call you when I have green light to interrogate him and we will do it together."

"OK Greg, I am sorry."

"No don't be, just let your anger out."

"I failed as a bodyguard," Goran lamented.

"No, you did what you could, it could have happened to any of us."

"I should have taken the stairs."

"They must have followed us and had back-up in the centre."

"I have to inform the police," Goran said.

"OK, I will drop you here and disappear. Keep us out of the picture, as usual."

"Right, stand by and have some of your men follow Susan and me when we drive home from the clinic."

"Let's switch cars then," Greg suggested and he took Susan's BMW and left the keys to his Datsun Patrol with Goran.

Susan's mind still remained in turmoil. Her best friend and soulmate shot, fighting for her life. The emergency doctor gave Susan an injection to counter her shock. She reclined in the waiting area into a soft chair and calmed down. She recalled the assassination, thinking the bullet had hit her, but it was Kathy who took the shot aimed at her. She applied mouth to mouth resuscitation until the ambulance arrived.

"We should have never moved outside our suite and gone shopping," she scolded herself. But this morning Kathy felt so happy and it was her day off, so one thing gave way to another, besides Kathy wanted to buy a present for Goran's birthday. The scenario of Kathy falling in protecting her and Goran's diving to bring them down to the floor, played in her mind. She still heard the hissing thud-thud of the shots. In playbacks they fell down in slow motion, as if they would make love but Kathy was still and her lips so lifeless, when she breathed air into her mouth to revive her.

Chapter Twenty Four
Goran

When Goran entered the clinic, he asked for Kathy and Susan. The duty nurse directed him to the waiting area for the emergency rooms. Goran saw Susan crouched on an easy chair and he touched her shoulder.

"Susan?"

"Oh Goran, thanks you are here." She started crying. Goran tried to calm her down and held her embraced. She pressed herself against him as if she would fear losing Kathy and also him. She saw Kathy and Goran at the breakfast table, Kathy telling them about her dream. Now she understood its meaning. The two forked street was Kathy and herself. With Kathy moving along the left street, she had to return to the same spot and then take the right street. Susan had a bad feeling and it tore her apart. 'Kathy," she whispered and Goran looked at her transformed face, her lips resembling Kathy's. He kissed her. Susan kissed him back, whispering 'Kathy!"

The door to the treatment room opened and the medical doctor treating Kathy emerged. Goran looked at him, but he shook his head. He came closer and took Susan's hand. "I am sorry," he said. Goran held Susan, who seemed collapsing. Tears streamed down from her eyes. He comforted her and gave her his handkerchief. Susan recovered again and stood up suddenly.

"I just want to go and say good-bye to her."

"I will come with you," Goran said and he left her alone with Kathy's body, waiting at the door. Susan pulled the cover from her head and bend down to kiss her. Goran came close and he stroked Kathy's cheek and covered her again.

"Let's drive home, Goran." She whispered. He held his arm out for her Susan took it and she walked with Goran from the clinic. Greg's car stood opposite the entrance. He held the car door open for her and then drove her home, followed by Greg and his driver in Susan's car. Susan said not a word as she still felt the heavy sedation she had received at the clinic. Goran helped her from the car and into the lift. He opened the door to her apartment, helped her to her bed, where Susan undressed and Goran assisted with her nightgown. Then he tucked her into bed and kissed her good night.

Goran kept busy washing dishes. He cleaned the kitchen and prepared himself a stiff scotch. He had not touched alcohol since his face transplant and the first sips ran like liquid fire to his stomach. It relaxed him. He checked on Susan, who had fallen asleep. He undressed, took a shower and cleaned thoroughly. He switched the music on and tuned into a station that played Greek music, reminding him of Kathy's favourites. He turned the steam on and sat down on the bench, enjoying the cleansing of his pores.

Suddenly a shadow hushed across the glazed shower doors and Susan appeared.

"May I join you?"

"Sure come in." Susan entered the low lit cubicle and closed the doors. "This is a great multifunctional unit," Goran praised her installation. Susan looked down at Goran who had been invigorated by the lower shower jets before.

"Not only your face looks great," she teased him. Goran enjoyed Susan, who could banter at any situation, save for today, when she collapsed in the aftermath of Kathy's assassination. He fidgeted on the plastic seat, while Susan sat down next to him and kissed him. Her hand wandered to his hardening penis and she enjoyed touching him. Kissing him gently, she moved across him and straddled him. At first lowering herself in slow motion and as soon as he moved slightly to help her into the love seat, she sighed, held on to the rails and started moving on him. Goran was in sweet agonies, but pictures of their lovemaking flashed through his mind. He felt how much Susan needed him now in absorbing the undeserved killing of Kathy. Goran enjoyed Susan's erotic attention, recalling earlier times when they were the first time together, with Kathy initiating a threesome. Goran had experienced an even more intense feeling with Kathy, when he was loved by them both, but Kathy remained his favourite woman, Susan's gasps brought him back from his daydreaming and he realized he had to give his heart to her, as Kathy would have wanted it and he intensified his counter movements to assure her of his love. He had to give all, as she danced on him, her breasts moving about him and her hardened nipples grazing his skin, enhancing the pleasures that started turning him on for her. It seemed to Goran as if Kathy had moved into Susan's body and he experienced similar sensations as he had with them both together, making love in Susan's wide bed. The slippery surface of their heated skins added an additional aphrodisiac. Sue's head snapped back as she started climaxing. He felt a signal that Kathy used to give him, a smack on his back.

But what he felt was Susan's one hand clasping his neck as she cried out and gasped. He felt his climax nearing and he increased his movements into her, pulling his buttock muscles together and Susan buckled and moaned, as if she would feel Goran's desperate moves to finally let go and become her man. Finally he started to heave himself more vehemently as he climaxed, Susan clambering to his body, her hands locked behind his neck, her hot breath on his neck.

"Ah Sue," Goran cried out. They stayed together for some time until their breathing returned to normal, when Susan loosened herself from Goran and she switched off the steam. She kissed Goran.

"Let's shower and go to bed." Goran nodded. He felt emotionally elated but a sweet tiredness had affected his knees, as he tried to stand up. He sat down again, while Susan adjusted the shower jets. The cold water had the effect of an instant wake and soon faded into pleasant warmth again that pervaded his body. Susan had stepped from the shower cabin and toweled herself off. She slipped into her nightgown and while Goran toweled off, she left for the bedroom. He followed her.

Susan lay in bed and sweet drowsiness pervaded her body. She thought of Goran's love that she felt as the greatest present Kathy had left her, a legacy that she had initiated with their first lovemaking many months before. Susan wondered how much Goran must have suffered, as he had an agony not being able to protect her from taking the assassin's deadly bullet. She had cried for the death of her soulmate, but she had come over it a great deal since she had made love to Goran. Doubting that he ever could replace Kathy, as he had suffered himself a great loss, she had been pleasantly surprised about the healing powers of Goran's love. The moment she climaxed she had seen both their ecstatic faces and she joined them with giving herself completely to Goran in a moment of intuition. Kathy, she thought, she will always be here for her and in her to share their unique love. She loved Goran, as if Kathy had asked her: Love him Susan, love him as much as you loved me. With thoughts about her satisfying climax, she drifted into deep sleep.

Goran felt a wonderful lightness he had not experienced since the days he had met Kathy and they had made love for the first time. He recalled his first important Tai Chi fight where he felt a similar feeling of lightness flying through the air in an attacking movement. He felt elevated floating on a cloud of happy content and many thoughts crossed his mind. He felt that he had loved Kathy much more than just being an initial love interest. Their love had matured and it reached a climax with her and Susan. This lightness had returned this evening making love to Susan, who had initiated it, much to the joy of himself and indeed as much to her own pleasure. The moment Susan threw her head back and climaxed, he had flashes of thoughts about love and death, centred on a discussion he had with Kathy the day of his accident, when he was in excruciating pain and being pulled from his burning sports car and noticing Kathy's appearance, her worried face and his pain reflected in her eyes and mimicry. Her permanent stay at his bedside gave him strength, as he felt her love going out to him wanting him to survive and get well again. He recalled Anne, her face merging with that of Kathy and when he saw Susan's face displaying her pleasure of loving him, he experienced this new woman with these faces merged into one. This face of a woman he loved now, Susan, who kissed him and wanted him most intimately with a great inner fire. She looked at him like all the faces of his lovers combined. He had felt a great sense of satisfaction, the moment Susan's fervent movements brought him to a climax. He buckled as Susan embraced him. "I love you Goran," she uttered the words in her breath and they touched him deep inside, as he drifted on a cloud into sleep.

Chapter Twenty Five
Chronis & May

Caltis' final fight is set for the afternoon and he appears to be more nervous although Chronis had given him his coca tea in the morning and yesterday three times. Something bothers him since two days, and he would not say a word to Chronis, but at times he paces around his quarters like a wounded leopard.

"Caltis you have to let steam off."

"Well, I am due for a warming up session in an hour's time."

"Have a few sips of tea."

"Later, I have still something to do. "

"Can I assist?"

"No. Fetch me in an hour's time." Caltis leaves and answers his mobile. It's May asking him to meet her in the café. Chronis finds her in the corner facing the terrace.

"Hi May." He kisses her. "What's up?" May looks concerned.

"I have to leave in an hour's time."

"Where to?"

"Back home." She looks at him with sad eyes,

"Oh, I thought…"

"That we stay here for the celebrations tonight after the finals?"

"Yes."

"That was the original plan."

"But..? Please tell me May, don't let me pull it word for word out of you."

"I overheard Robin's trainer urging him to leave. "

"Why that?"

"There was a rumor circulating between the trainers that Olivia had been involved with spiking her uncle's drink and therefore he lost his bout."

"Oh damned!"

"Of course now they are looking soon for me as I was Olivia's only contact, besides her family."

"But how did they find that out?"

"Her uncle mistreated her and she talked. He is a mean guy and he beat her up."

"What a bad ending…" Chronis mused. "I hope they keep it to themselves until the tournament has ended."

"You must not say anything if there are enquiries." She stood up. "I have to go now." Chronis stood up and hugged her. "Keep in touch Chronis." She kissed him and left. Chronis stood for a moment wrapped up in the bad news and pictures of their happy times flashed through his mind. Then he settled down and rushed to his quarters to write mail to Castor, who had not reported back to him for some time. As soon as he finished his email to his friend, Castor's report arrived on his laptop: Dear Chronis, matters are in turmoil here. However, let me start. Some days ago a group of security men had taken Takis prisoner and our men followed them, but lost them as if swallowed up by the earth. They must have taken Takis to a safe house, we are still searching for. We have found out that these security men's leader is linked to Goran, who is staying at a secure outbuilding of the Clinic where he was treated for his burns. We thought that Goran has given up on his clubs, but somebody called K&S enterprises has bought up all available shares on Goran's MAC-company that controls the Martial Arts Clubs. Freeing Takis, as discussed with Caltis, would only be possible to kidnap one of the surgeons under whose care Goran is at present. You must not be mad at me, but Caltis asked me to keep this conversation confidential until he gives orders otherwise. Yesterday we had finally cornered the two women with Goran and as a kidnapping attempt was botched, our sharpshooter had understood to shoot and wound the woman surgeon. But instead he shot the other woman, who moved at that instant and she died in hospital. Goran and his security group chased our wounded man and took him to their secure and safe compound. In short Chronis, we are fucked! The Don is looking out for Takis, as he took money from Nasos that belonged to him, and Goran and his men will get all info from our man, who will be forced to talk, I have to go now. Take care and support Caltis to win or get a place in today's final bout. All the best, Castor.

The news hit Chronis like a tidal wave and he felt smacked in the face. Caltis had not discussed with him matters of security and after all he acted like a gangster shooting a girlfriend of Goran. He had started an unnecessary war that the Don will profit from. After all, he, Chronis, was in charge of security matters and second in command after Takis, besides Takis would have agreed with him in tackling these matters differently. Now one word to the press and the police would swarm all over the place and investigate, finding out about Caltis' fixing of the sports car racing, where Goran's car had been badly tampered with. By now the investigations of the insurance company had already yielded foul play, but fortunately Iannis the fixer had been shot dead and Susan, his girlfriend and accessory to it had disappeared. Chronis feared that the Don had a hand in all of it and that sooner or later Takis would be next on his list and then?

Caltis had been uneasy for these last two fights of the championships. The capture of Takis and the killing of Goran's girlfriend weighed down on him. Since Takis had been taken, his gang under the leader Castor had nothing but bad news to report. He could not throw the towel in now and abandon his big dream of a title, besides he would look suspicious if there would be an investigation about the Armenian's performance. He had not heard anything from Chronis, but then he would not discuss matters of his gang with him, as here Chronis had to concentrate on assisting him to win the championships, besides he had used Chronis' relationship to May, to get close to his opponent and through May's girlfriend to spike the burly man's energy drink. It had worked well, but now in the finals he had to rely on his skills. He estimated his present strength at 90 percent, but he hoped that the coca teas Chronis brewed him would stimulate him to unlock the missing ten percent. He prepared himself for the warm up session and called on Chronis.

"I am ready, we have to go."

"I will come and fetch you." Chronis was fed up with the egocentric and stubborn Caltis. First he had not entrusted him with information about happenings with the gang and secondly did not consult him for possible solutions. He had broken my trust in him. How would I continue working for him? Chronis considered winding down and converse with his girlfriend. Chronis accompanied Caltis to the warm up area part to the main hall where the finals would take place. His mind was on May and he ignored Caltis, once he had entered the change rooms. He activated his cellphone.

"May where are you?"

"I am in the Quartier Latin." She murmured the name of a hotel Chronis did not catch. "Are you free tonight?"

"Yes, I could get away."

"Ok, let's meet later. I will call you when I am finished here."

"OK." She cut her phone.

Chronis had no specific grounds to stay during the finals, except to join Caltis' staff, as he had to appear as his official aide. As with most finals the fighting usually bored him, with the opponents being careful to gain points and avoid taking unnecessary risky movements. When the announcements ended and the hall filled with people, Chronis took his seat amongst the staff members who greeted him. He replied absentmindedly thinking about May and a romantic night, before flying back with Caltis' entourage to Athens. He felt drained and disappointed and could not care about the outcome of the fight. He had a notion, when watching the English opponent of Caltis that the sinewy fighter would be difficult to beat, His displayed movements were smooth and sharp in their conclusion. He definitely had an edge on Caltis, who had perhaps enough physical skills to equal those of his opponent, but he lacked the inner concentration and balance, 'the inner chi'. To be a true champion one had to achieve a balance with the outer, physical one.

Caltis had difficulties concentrating on his fight. He appeared on edge, had a few moments of brilliance, but fell behind on points and neglected the aesthetic quality of his movements. The Englishman deserved definitely to be ahead. However, suddenly Caltis soared with his attacks and he drew even with his opponent, much to Chronis' surprise. The Greek camp gave him great vocal support, but the English side booed. It seemed that Caltis had become extremely aggressive and intimidated his opponent. These tackles changed from vehement pushing of hands to quick turns and kicks, which Caltis was known for. Initially he charged successfully, until his opponent had retaliated with a counter attack that proved effective and

Caltis fell behind. He started to fight dirty and his opponent's side protested. The effect of the coca had softened, Caltis thought as the English visitors booed. Time was up and the fighters were equal on points. Extra time had been given to find a winner. When the English fighter advanced in points, a tumult broke out between groups of supporters for the fighters and in the follow up of noise and fistfights the championships were stopped. The Greek fans battled with the security guards, who were incapable to squash the aggressive fights between the two main supporting groups of their champions.

For the jurors it was a clear win for the English fighter, who was ahead on points after extra time had been given and the fight had to be stopped due to hooliganism, which was unheard up to now on any events. Security cleared the hall and the instigators of the public disturbance were taken into custody by the arriving police.

Chronis had enough. He excused himself by his colleagues and left, as soon as he saw Caltis losing the fight. He was no longer interested in witnessing this drab and boring fight, lacking any spirit, especially from Caltis. He had relied too much on the coca tea to burst his energy like in the semifinals, but he looked like a fighter without a soul. Chronis phoned May, who answered immediately. "I will be at Café Deux Magots in twenty minutes,"

"Caltis did not win?"

"No."

"I will wait for you inside at the back," May said.

"OK." Chronis closed his mobile and rushed to the taxi ranks.

Chapter Twenty Six
Greg

Greg had been driving with Bill, his man skilled in electronics, to check on Sue's security installation. The guard at Susan's clinic had raised the alarm and Greg would adhere immediately to the warning signals, as this could be part for another attack. However, when they arrived at Susan's compound, they found that somebody had cut a wire in the electric fence and shot at an observation camera. Greg called his men guarding the safe house, but there was no reply. He ordered his men back again, sensing this incident as deviation tactics.

Goran and Sue had a meeting with Susan's investment advisor, who looked after their combined funds in K&S Investments. His shareholdings had been transferred to Kathy and Susan, who had agreed to look after it, while he had to undergo treatment for his face. The investments did well, as part of K&S Investments had been invested into a portfolio where income from the sports car racing bet had bolstered the portfolio. It had served well to pay for the services of Greg and his bills at Susan's clinic. The investment looked prosperous and the funds invested into the sports bet on Elena, had provided them with a windfall.

Goran had a substantial sum transferred to his private account. He had news that Caltis had lost the championships, had been ridiculed as an unclean fighter and he was outraged that Takis had been captured by security men, who were linked to him. Goran expected his fight with Caltis to intensify on all levels. Even if the insurance company for his sports car had found tampering with it, mechanical wear and tear and mechanical failure exempted them to pay him for a replacement, as they had been discussing with his lawyer. Goran needed more proof. He contacted Greg, who was on his way back to the safe house, informing him about the incident at Susan's clinic, which had been taken care of.

When Greg and his men arrived at their safe house, they had been alerted by red light. Having their weapons ready, they surrounded the safe house. Two of his men had been shot. Greg called for their medical man who took care of the one guard who was still alive. The man could be stabilized and he certainly could identify the intruders. When they entered the cell where Takis had been kept, the room was empty. A big opening had been broken into the floor exposing a storm water pipe, big enough to get Takis freed. "Damned!" Greg shouted, "get fingerprints, something we could nail these bastards on." There were bloodspots on the floor. Somebody had been wounded from the intruders, or perhaps it was Takis. Two men went through the storm water pipe to follow the escape route. Meanwhile the medical man had done a great job and the wounded man could talk.

"Mob men," he said. Greg immediately contacted Goran, whose father knew the whereabouts of the Don.

"Dad? It's Goran.

"Hello son. What's up?"

I need to speak to the Don."

"That's not easy "

"He kidnapped Takis from Greg's safe house."

"Well, what will you achieve talking to him?"

"He broke into our property and stole my prisoner."

"Well, I better come with you."

"OK Dad." While Greg drove to the location, his crew, armored to the teeth, arrived in good time and two his scouts confirmed the location, where the blood spots had stopped, quite close to the Don's residence. The Don was alerted and expected Goran and his Dad at the entrance gates. The guard let them through. Goran asked Greg on standby, and only act on his command. Don's men accompanied them into the marble hall of the residence.

"You must wait here," the guard said.

"Come in, Walt," the Don greeted Goran's Dad.

"Hi Don, long time no see."

"Indeed."

"This is my son Goran."

"Ah the Tai Chi fighter."

"Yes."

"Well you did not come for a social visit alone," the Don continued. "However, as we are civilized people, we have a drink first. Do you care to join me for tea?" Typical Don, he could never give up the tradition of tea -time, having been educated in England, Walt mused.

"Yes, that would be nice Don." Goran nodded. Don sensed his anger.

"May I begin, having done our social niceties?" Goran said.

"By all means," Don replied, "What's the problem?"

"You took one of our prisoners, shooting one man and killing the other."

"Wait a moment, I do not understand." Walt mediated immediately "It's Takis."

"OH the one who robbed me?"

"Well we captured him for my rehabilitation at court."

"I am confused." Don said and then listened to Goran outlining the story of the shooting of his girlfriend Kathy and threatening Susan and her clinic, who gave him a second chance for life. The Don listened carefully. He asked for more tea and then explained his perspective of what had happened to Goran.

"Do you see we need him as a crown witness?" Goran said.

"No, you have Caltis to deal with, who masterminded your accident. See?" Goran suddenly saw the whole picture unwinding in front of his mind's eyes.

"We took care of Iannis, he cheated on us." Don said. "We took Takis, as he took money which belonged to us and he has to return it."

"I would need him to get to Caltis," Goran said. The Don looked serious.

"We were not aware that the men holding him were connected closer to you." Don replied.

"We have to resolve this satisfactory to all parties," Walt said and Don nodded.

"Well, as I cannot give you Takis back, I owe you and we will take Caltis out for you."

"He is mine," Goran said hastily.

"All right." Don smiled. "I guess you have an old score to settle first." Walt sighed.

"Could I have a word with you in private?" Don stood up and Walt followed him.

"I understand you are worried about your son, Walt. He had been badly dealt with."

"It nearly cost him his life and he went through living hell."

"Indeed. I tell you what. We are going back a long time and I can see that this Caltis and his men are ripping your clubs off and they behave like despots and all they are, we call cowards and sons-of-bitches."

"My son needs his club back and his rightful place as a champion."

"Yes, he is a good boy. All I can promise you is a back-up of your son in his fight against Caltis, even if we stay officially in the background, we will make sure the better man will win." Walt smiled; his old army friend would never let him down.

"Walt?"

"Yes?"

"Listen, for the shootout at the safe house, I apologize, it was botched. We will make a delivery of necessary weapons for the security men. "

"Thanks Don." Walt emerged and convinced Goran that the deal with Don stood. Goran did not like it, but he accepted it. It certainly made sense not to be with Don on bad terms, besides his mind had concentrated on his tactics to fight Caltis on his return. Don came to say good bye to them and addressed Goran.

"You look like a young god, I must say whoever did surgery on you will be always on my books. "

"It's Susan, a friend of mine, she owns the J&S Clinic for maxillofacial and facial replacement surgery."

"She has done an excellent job, congratulations."

"Thanks." Father and son left Don's residence accompanied by his security guards, who seemed permanently alert.

Goran spoke to Greg that he may relax and that he will see him tomorrow for his training and a strategic session. Then he drove his Dad home discussing with him basic strategies.

"I need to win against Caltis the smart way."

"You need back up, which we have secured now."

"I need to get our club back."

"Sure, I have been buying up shares slowly, Walt said." Goran looked surprised.

"Well, Susan and I have with you together still the majority, but just, as I had lots of expanses."

"Not just, I have increased it and we own now 55 percent, meaning we have a majority."

"Wow that is great." Goran swallowed.

"Happy birthday Goran!"

"Thanks Dad." He hugged Walt as he accompanied his father to the door of his residence.

"We'll keep in touch." Goran had neglected his father in the past and he felt that he owed him a lot, especially as he worked quietly in the background, preparing the solid ground that would hold him up in his fight for justice and for his rights. He made a mental note to speak to his father more often, especially as he lived alone, a recluse writing his memoir. Since his mother had died in a car accident some years back, Walt had preferred to withdraw from public life. Goran only saw him when he came for general meetings of shareholders at the annual event. Kathy liked to talk to him and he appreciated her. Yet he became a different man since Goran had his accident and Walt supported Kathy, as he feared that she would break looking at his burned and disfigured face. But Kathy remained at Goran's bedside crying her eyes out, until she found the extraordinary surgeon, Susan, who gave Goran a new taste for life.

Chapter Twenty Seven
Caltis

Caltis group had been disappointed by the second place of their competing Tai Chi fighter and prepared to leave Paris. Besides, Caltis had been given notice by the championship board that an investigation into the rumors of fight fixing at the semifinals had been set into motion. Until this had been resolved, the results of the fights would not be final.

The group arrived at the airport and faced protesters from the fans of the Armenian, who shouted at Caltis and his team, carrying banners in two languages, calling him names and asking him to stand down. His team finally boarded their plane back to Athens. Caltis felt tired and burned out, an indifferent attitude to the botched attempt to secure a championship in Tai Chi, meant for him now the end of a once promising career. He dropped into the seat next to one of his men and having taken a tranquilizer, he fell immediately asleep.

Chronis had chosen to sit next to another group of Caltis' staff, where he would be left to his musing and chasing thoughts about his future. He had felt the brunt of a two way street of harsh criticism, one from the protesters and hooligans from his country and second from Caltis, who scolded his disinterest for the final fight complaining the lack of his attention. He deserved to lose, Chronis thought, dirty tactics and low standard of Tai chi fighting on his part, what did Caltis expect from that, top honours? Chronis thought of May and he pulled his mobile phone from his pocket. He composed an SMS, strains of romance lingered in his mind, as he tried to find equivalent words in English, while the airplane started rolling toward the take-off strip. He finished the message in a hurry, pressed the send button and immediately switched his gizmo off, just as announcement was made in that regard.

Caltis and his staff were not celebrated on their arrival at E. Venizelos airport. The rumours of fight fixing and dirty fighting had already preceded his homecoming, spreading like wildfire. Caltis knew he was finished as an upcoming Tai Chi fighter and had taken the wrong path, avoiding tougher training. He had to blame himself, but then emotions welled up in him with

feelings of hate for Goran, he blamed for everything: The man's arrogance and know-it-all attitude, his liaison with pretty women, who were
out only for a share of his wealth and success
with the Martial Arts Clubs. When he chose
Kathy for a mistress, Caltis saw his opportunity
to stop Goran's steep success and cut a share
off for himself. As Kathy was related to Takis,
his best friend from times in the army, a plan
started to shape in his mind to deal with his opponent once and for all. Takis disliked the
'Golden Boy' of Tai Chi fighting and he joined
Caltis, who formed a new club from ex- army
friends.

"You should have trained harder," a voice of an
onlooker brought him back to reality. He saw a
face he knew from before but he could not put a
name to. As the man snapped some pictures he
recalled having seen him snooping around the
club and accompanying a cameraman wherever Caltis had been present in a club competition.
As the minibus stopped at the clubhouse, he
recalled his name, 'Franco'. He linked up with
Kathy, who was dead and it was the responsibility of his men. "Stupid Castor," he mumbled
and had immediately commanded him to assemble the gang in the old windmill tonight,

"Chronis?"

"Yes Castor, what's up?"

"You better be here for our meeting at the safe house tonight."

"I was not aware of it, having to attend a family funeral."

"Oh, I am sorry." Castor said, "But Caltis asked me for organizing the meeting."

"That's all right, if matters of security come up, tell me and I will deal with them later."

"Yes, I will do that."

"Apologies to Caltis, but I could not reach him on his mobile." Castor cut the connection. It's not surprising at all, Chronis mused that Caltis had taken on Castor as his new aide and personal assistant. In a way this suited him, as his mind had been entrenched in leaving Caltis and his ex-army buddies, especially as Takis had been captured by the Don and would never come back. Without Takis, Chronis would never have support in Caltis' gang. He dressed up in his dark suit, donned a protective overcoat and helmet, started his Yamaha motorbike and raced toward Piraeus for the funeral. The air was cold and swooshed past him blowing at his overalls. The moment he slowed down and entered the suburb of Piraeus, a different atmosphere greeted him. He drove through familiar lanes and streets and recalled them from his early childhood that seemed to come back to him. He parked his motorbike at his aunt's house and joined the family members assembled for the funeral. "Hello Chronis," a young brunette woman approached him.

"Hi Susanna," long time no see." She smiled and her face reminded him of another woman.

"Maybe we could catch up after the funeral."

"Yes sure, we will."

Caltis drove to the safe house of his gang. The windmill looked like a ghost against the night sky, with whorls of dark clouds gathering at a distance. "A storm coming up," he thought aloud to Castor, who drove the 4x4 vehicle.

"The weather news had predicted a thunderstorm."

"It will be synonymous for this meeting," Caltis murmured, then added "Have all confirmed to be here?"

"Only Chronis hasn't."

"What's wrong with him?"

"He had to go to a funeral."

"He could have called me." Caltis became angry.

"He told me that he tried to phone you, but your mobile had been engaged."

"Yeah, the lawyers are crawling all over me like ants." Castor parked the car alongside all other vehicles from members of their gang. It appeared to him that all would be present.

Castor called for order and read the agenda and then Caltis took he chair.

"I have called an urgent meeting, as matters concerning the Martial Arts Club and our CATA organization will need restructuring to deal with most pressing matters." Murmuring erupted and Castor called for order. Caltis continued. "As you know our number two and financial expert, Takis, had been taken hostage by a security gang linked to Goran and his men. We will take them and squeeze the living daylight out of them." The brothers-in-crime voiced their confirmation and Caltis paused. "However, meanwhile Don's people have captured Takis, taken him away, right under the noses of their original captors, I call pussycats!" The comrades roared with laughter and Takis sensed he had a chance to insert feelings of confidence, revenge and bloodlust into his gang of ex-army men and comrades. He rasped.

"I do not want to bore with a long speech. I need volunteers to go after Takis and rescue him from Don's clutches. It is possible to take on a house occupied with gangsters, as we have equally effective weapons and skills we practiced in the army. Let's refresh them and strike into the heart of the enemy!" The comrades, thirsty for using all the weapons, stashed away below the floorboards of the windmill, had been turned on by Caltis stirring speech for action promised to them for a long time.

"The time has arrived. We will attack tomorrow at dawn. Castor will discuss the strategic plan and form groups of two. Any volunteers to check out the enemy's place?" All raised their hands. Castor decided for straws to be drawn. He took a box of matches ad shortened one of them. The two men selected were given instructions and fighting gear, two way radios and a new mobile phone for urgent and secretive communication back to Castor. The two men changed into their battle gear and donned their knapsack with ammunitions and surveillance gear and exited the safe house. They changed the number plate on the Nissan 4x4, which had been prepared by Castor with reserve petrol and tools and drove away, their satellite positioning gizmo pointing the way.

Chronis has been informed by Castor about the meeting and that two of their comrades were on their way to scout for the place where Takis was held imprisoned. "Come on Chronis, have a drink," statuesque Susanna approached him, "after all we want to wish our cousin a happy journey."

"Indeed," Chronis agreed, "Why not? I just had to talk to my friend, I have not seen for a while."

"Is he part of the MAC?" The question caught Chronis by surprise. How did Susanna know this?

"Have you been at the MAC lately?"

"Yes, I know a member who took me there."

"Hey Susi," he heard as a young man approached them.

"Chronis, this is Nestor my boyfriend." They shook hands and he invited them for a drink.

"As we are all cousins somewhere, let's check out the buffet."

"I am rather for a drink," Chronis said and Susanna joined him.

"May I call you Susi?"

"Perhaps later, when we'll know each other better." They all got on well with each other and decided to visit a trendy discotheque nearby.

The suburb of Piraeus is one of the oldest suburbs in Athens and Susanna listened to her new friend Chronis, she felt attracted to. Not alone through his knowledge about the city of her mother's choice, but also due to the fact that they both had Greek mothers, while their fathers were Germans. It's no coincidence, Chronis thought, while driving to the address of the nightclub. Susanna asked him about his childhood and he described the Piraeus he grew up in, rich in history, which one could feel at every turning of streets, on the great central square, and of course at the harbour areas. Chronis found a parking spot near the disco and with the others arriving, they entered the dancing and night club. Chronis asked Susanna for a dance.

"How come I have never seen you before Susanna?"

"My parents insisted that I have higher education in England and Germany."

"You did well; you have a command of at least three languages."

"Well let's see: Greek from Mom, yes, German from Dad, and English at school." She laughed. "But my English is worse than my German." Chronis started falling in love with Susanna. He pulled her closer at a slow-dance and Susanna seemed to enjoy it. I will make love to her tonight, Chronis mused and smiled.

"You seem to be happy, what are you smiling about?"

"I intend to charm you so long tonight, until I can call you Susi." She laughed. Chronis loved to see her laugh and it turned him on.

Chapter Twenty Eight
Susanna

When photographs from Chronis and Susanna, appeared on his facebook site, Caltis, alarmed by Castor, is looking at Susan. "It can't be," he murmurs and phones Chronis immediately.

"Hallo Caltis, what's up?"

"Are you at your laptop?"

"Yes."

"Go and open your facebook site. "

"Yes, and now?"

"Who is the woman you are with?" Chronis feels a bout of anger in the pit of his stomach. "It's my friend Susanna. Is there a problem?"

"Well, let's say there would be one soon." Chronis panics.

"What about her?"

"I need you to come with her to a meeting."

"All right, when?"

"Come to my place for brunch."

"I will see if Susanna is available." Chronis felt that something was the matter with such an urgent visit to be arranged to see Caltis. He wondered what it could be, as he dialed Susanna's number. She listened to his talk, as she intended to enter the General Hospital, where she had an interview. She agreed to come and Chronis supposed to fetch her in an hour's time.

He thought hard about any link and cause, why he had to bring Susanna to Caltis' offices. He dialed the CATA number and confirmed the appointment with Caltis.

While Chronis drove with Susanna to their appointment with Caltis, she asked him continually the reason for her requested presence, but he could not offer her any reasonable answer.

"It's probably for an interview." Chronis muttered.

"Yes, but what for?" Susanna carried on bugging him, but Chronis talked around the issue. Although he did not know what this visit was about, he tried hard to put Susanna's mind at rest.

Caltis' residence had been an old station building he had bought through a friend, with connections to the railway authorities, who had since constructed new lines on different tracks and the 19th century building had been neglected and declared useless, but Caltis could make good use of the meter thick walls that acted like a shield.

His guards guided the couple into the entrance hall. The building looked impressive with the magnificent high entrance into a high volume hall with a glazed vaulted roof closure.

"I always love to see the sky." Caltis greeted them, as he observed them looking up.

"It's magnificent." Susanna said. Chronis introduced her to Caltis.

"It is most fortunate for us all that Chronis has brought you here today." He said and walked ahead to show the way to his offices.

"Chronis spoke about you and your organization."

"I hope you heard good things."

"Indeed, of course I am curious why I am here."

"Let's say that I have an offer you can't refuse."

"That sounds dangerous," Susanna prodded.

"Wait!" Caltis said and he checked for any signs of being overheard. He started off to compliment Susanna and ask her if she would be willing to impersonate another person for a short time. The pay was good. As Susan had some experience with amateur theatre, she was an ideal candidate in the organization of Caltis' family business.

"I need you and your acting talents for an important mission."

"Could you tell me more about it?"

"It is still in the conceptual stage, but I will have you planted into the J&S Clinic for a short while." Susanna swallowed, she knew that the woman running he clinic looked like her. Rumour had it that she was her half-sister, but as her mother had died at her birth and her father had soon after disappeared, she had not known about it. She was three years old when her aunt took her into her family.

"What would be my role?"

"You have to act as Susan, not as Susanna."

"Do I look like her?" What about my voice?"

"We will show you videos and voice recordings, you have to study and practice. "

"Well, I have no idea how to stay undetected, as I am not a surgeon."

"I know. All you have to do is to stay in her office and prepare for a seminar."

"Well, I will have to read medical journals?" Susan sighed.

"We will have you covered in case somebody suspects anything. For now take the videos and practice and come back at night."

"All right!" She shook Caltis; hand.

As the matter seemed to be an easy job, acting as a doctor, she had been trained as a nurse and at home in the medical environment. She accepted the job and the beneficial payment, with a few thousand Euros as down payment. As a friend of Chronis, she was accepted as being part of Caltis' family, as he also became responsible for her dutiful performance of the job offered.

Chronis felt tricked into something he would have not agreed to, if Caltis' would not have powers that reached the families of most of his comrades. Now it was his turn, but Chronis felt a chance to rehabilitate himself with the leader and regain his power position as number two. Yet, he had a bad feeling in the pit of his stomach. Perhaps if he knew more about the matter with Susanna, he would have still time to make up his mind and decide if he wished to pursue his career with the dusky faced tyrant. He rather would coach Susanna and help her, as she would need all support to live up to her role and as he had fallen in love with her, all his efforts were actually their combined efforts and the funds earned a good basis for starting off together. Only thing, he mused, he still had to secure her love for him and that would take time. But this opportunity to be close to her most of the time, seemed the chance he had been waiting for. It was to him a gift from the gods. He drove towards town.

"What do you think Chronis, can I make it?"

"Of course you can, why?"

"I have no video player."

"In that case you have to come to my place."

"All right." Chronis smiled, he had indeed a good opportunity to seduce her now." He drove into his garage and closed the roller door as soon as he stopped his car. He showed Susanna the way and set up the video player. Susanna watched the video, while Chronis fetched a bottle of wine.

"My god, how will I do this?" Susanna leaned back on the settee and repeated Susan's words on the video, trying hard imitating the surgeon who looked astonishing similar in her facial structure to her. Besides she had the eyebrows and eyes as if she would look at herself. She experienced fear of failure, but at the same time she felt a rising thrill that she would have the power, impersonating somebody so similar to herself, fooling everybody. And Susanna believed that she would succeed. After all, behind those rumours of being half-sisters there might be at least a physical resemblance.

"You will do just fine," Chronis encouraged her. He handed her some wine.

"To your success!" They toasted each other.

"To you Chronis for helping me." She raised her glass again.

"Thank you and to us to make it happen!" Susanna had swallowed her wine, as she became increasingly nervous thinking about this evening, when she had to present herself as Susan to be approved in appearance, body language and voice, by Caltis. As Chronis fetched more wine, she stood up and took her glass.

"We supposed to drink to our friendship," she said and hooked her arm through his, a central European custom.

"All right Susanna."

"You have to drink with me at the same time and drink all." Chronis followed her.

"Now we supposed to kiss." Chronis took her empty glass and placed it together with his on the table. Then he placed his arm around her waist and kissed her. She responded to his kiss and a warm feeling rose from the pit of his belly and spread to his face. He was in love. As she separated from him, he wished to carry on.

"We have to go through the video tapes again and you have to check on me."

"Yes," Chronis whispered as his emotions ran high. He wanted to make love to her now. She sensed it and smiled.

"We have to view the video tapes again Chronis."

"All right Susanna," he said.

"You may call me Susan from now on," she laughed imitating Susan's laugh on the tapes. It startled Chronis.

"OK, Susan. That laugh had been just like the one on the tape."

"Tell me, really?" She teased him. He came close and sat down next to her, his leg touching

hers. He kissed her and she moved her leg onto his. It aroused him.

"I want you Susan," he said.

"We will have time for that later." She replied
businesslike, switched on the video again and
practiced Susan's gesticulation, the way she
moved her head and spoke with a low voice.

"It's time to go," Chronis said, who had reclined
on the wide settee and watched Susan's exercises, walk and body movements.

"OK, I am ready for the test performance."
Chronis took his shoulder holster, placed his
gun inside and donned his leather jacket. He let
Susan leave first, then he activated his alarm
with his remote.

Chapter Twenty Nine
Susanna

Goran has trained as a guest at the club, using
the name of Agor and he is back in top form,
yet keeping a low profile. Befriending the new
secretary at reception, who had registered him
for a visitor's permit, he obtains a list of the
members which he will check out with the help
of Greg. Finishing his workout, he returns to
Susan's quarters. Driving along the seaside

suburbs, he stops at a shopping area. He would surprise her and prepare dinner. He walks to a greengrocer's stall and selects some fruit and vegetables.

Caltis has tested Susanna's impersonation, lauded her efforts and accepted her act as satisfactory to work for the time needed, to complete his sinister plan. He hands Susanna an envelope and she is over the moon with the generous down payment.
"Be ready for tonight!" Chronis has to get you close to the clinic. Stay in the car, until I come!"
Caltis moves with Castor backing him up into the vicinity of the clinic. Since Goran had recovered, he has not seen him around, as he does not know his new face. However, at the club a new visitor's permit had been requested by a man called Agor and he might be Goran with a new identity.
As Susan is close to her home, she notices a Car across the road and a man lying on the ground. She stops her car and investigates the body.
"An accident here?" she murmurs. She bends over the body and checks it in the beam of her car's lights. Suddenly she feels to hands grabbing her neck and a needle pierces her arm.

While she passes out she heard a familiar voice. "Get her into my car!"

Susanna is nervous as the time drags on. Chronis pacifies her, caressing her thigh. She feels stirred by his attention and kisses him.
"It's time to go!" Caltis had appeared. "Move over, I drive." He stops at Susan's car and briefs Susanna to become consciously Susan. "Change your jackets, hurry up! Get to her parking. Here are the keys to Susan's house. Goran will be there cooking a meal. Be aware that you have to inject him with this syringe, at an opportune moment." He hands her Susan's bag. "Everything's there, as we have discussed. Now get going!" Susanna slips into Susan's jacket and Castor slips a lifeless Susan into Susanna's jacket. He asks Chronis to be ready to visit Susanna, as soon as she signals him, as an outpatient for eventualities. Then he joins Castor who drives him to the safe house, where Susan is to be held.
Chronis drives home, assured that Susanna will call him. He looks forward to visiting her at the clinic.

Caltis gang drove Susan to the safe house, where she is taken into the uppermost floor and tied to a chair. She has bruises on her hands from the rough handling of Caltis' gang. Castor touches her and is attracted to her. He loosens her ties and supports her head on the wooden beam behind her chair. She reminds him of his late mother.

Susanna has driven Susan's car into the garage, using the remote control on the keys Caltis has handed her. She checks Susan's handbag and uses her lipstick to raise no suspicions. Once she has completed the ritual she has observed on the video tapes, she moves from the car and walks from the side entrance into the hall. The smell of cooking wafts to her from the kitchen. She drops her shoes and slips into sandals as Susan used to do.

"Hi Susan," Goran greets from the kitchen where he busies himself.

"Hi Goran, you prepared dinner?"

"I am ready soon."

"Oh it's a surprise." She is relived that he is busy and had no time to scrutinize her yet. He has not noticed a difference in her voice, thank god. While Goran made his last preparations for dinner, Susanna sets the table mats and places cutlery. She waited with the glasses, as Goran had opened a bottle of wine. She dimmed the lights and lit a candle, she saw on the side table.

"Ah, a romantic evening." He came close to her. Susanna's heartbeat increased. He kissed her.

"Oh fantastic," she exclaimed as he served a shrimp salad. He smiled and brought two glasses and the wine. He poured her and then himself.

"To our health," she said and toasted with him. She had rehearsed that from the video. "Indeed," he said. "That reminds me, I running short of medication."

"I'll see to it," Susanna said and tasted the shrimp salad.

"You like it?"

"Mh," she murmured, "excellent." They ate in silence. Susanna dared not to talk too much as she was afraid to make a faux pas.

"And now for the main dish," he announced. Goran brought the food in a covered porcelain dish. He opened the lid. "Voila!" Susanna's eyes had a flicker of contraction, as she tried to remember Susan's favourite dish. Then she sighed, as she recalled having seen the same dish and heard Susan's exclamation.

"Ah, Nasi Goreng, how wonderful Goran." He smiled like a schoolboy, who had pleased his Mom, cooking the favourite dish for her birthday. They ate in silence while Goran made small talk and explained to her his training sessions.

"You are taciturn today, Susan." He said and she recoiled inside. She had to be alert. "I am tired today," she sighed.

"Your seminar presentation?"

"Indeed, it's draining me more than I thought."

"OK, relax." He poured her more wine. "Cheers."

"Cheers," she repeated and sipped some of it. She had to be careful and stay sober, as it was soon time to retire, be ready with the syringe and inject the tranquilizer into him.

"For desert?" He looked at her. She understood that he was keen to make love to her. She had to play along. This was a golden opportunity to do what she had been asked to do.

"Ah Goran, I see that naughty look in your eyes." She had made a faux pas, as this line had not been in her videos, but she had taken a chance. He smiled.

"I will take a shower," she said and got up help-ing him carry some of the dishes.

"I will do the dishes," he said, 'go and have your shower. He looked at her again and Susanna panicked that he had detected something he knew from Susan and that she had missed out doing it. She tilted her head to the side and this seemed to have reassured him again. She smiled and went to the bedroom.

She had to be careful checking out Susan's wardrobe. She remembered her turquoise business suite; which Susan preferred to wear to the clinic. Fortunately today she had worn the dark blue outfit and Susanna had the jacket changed, as she had the exact pants in the same colour. She slipped out of her clothes and changed into Susan's bathrobe. Damned, she had forgotten her handbag, but she would fetch it later, when Goran took a shower. She put Susan's shower cap on her head and could not wait to experience the all over jets that massaged her skin from the adjustable water spray and aroused her. She sat down on the bench and relaxed. Suddenly she jumped up. If Goran would enter the shower while she was here, he would detect a scar from her appendix operation. Caltis did not know that. She switched the shower off and dried herself in a hurry, donning the bathrobe and hurrying into the bedroom, where she slipped into Susan's silken pajamas and nightgown. She heard Goran switching on TV, while he cleaned the dishes and she hoped that Susan's kidnapping had not yet been discovered. She reclined on Susan's comfortable bed and relaxed, thinking about her task ahead. After some time Goran switched the TV off and went to the bathroom to have a shower. It was time to act. She went on tiptoes to fetch her bag,

Susan's bag, where she had placed the syringe. She positioned the open bag behind the generous cushion, dimmed the lights and went to bed, simulating to be asleep. She heard Goran shower with the music on. The monotonous noise made her sleepy and she closed her eyes. As the music stopped she pinched herself to stay awake. She must not sleep now! She talked to herself without making a sound.

Goran showered and felt happy like a lark. The wine had relaxed him together with his successful dinner that delighted Susan. She looked to him younger today, but then he felt younger himself too and her smile made him feel wanted and he intended to complete what he had wanted all evening, talking and building up tension. She might be tired, he thought, but never for making love. Since Kathy's death, she had changed, turned around completely and enjoyed sex with him. He dried carefully and slipped into his nightgown, he soon would ditch anyway.

Susan saw Goran entering the bedroom. He looked gorgeous, she thought. She would not enjoy his sexual attentions, as she had to knock him out with a potent tranquilizer shot. Damned, she thought as he approached her, slipping below the lightweight cover. "Are you asleep Susan?" He touched her. Her body reacted immediately, and the more he caressed her the more she became aroused.

"Ah, Goran," she sighed and played along. There had to be no trouble now to spoil the lovemaking. He kissed her and she responded. He became aroused as he held her breast and stroked her hardened nipple, while she moved toward his penis. He seemed to be highly aroused as he turned her again and entered her from behind. She held back and tried to think what to do but let him tire first and spend himself. She moved against him and this seemed to drive him toward his climax. It took a while with his movements to become harder and faster. Finally he cried out as she breathed heavily and came with him. "Ah Goran, my man." She knew that from the video. "Oh Susan how good, how good..." he sighed and seemed to be drifting off into a slumber. She waited with baited breath until he had let her loose and she turned to retrieve the syringe from her bag behind her cushion. He moaned a bit and she waited again. Then she primed the needle until drops appeared. She positioned the needle to his shoulder muscle and injected with a perfect stab emptying the syringe without waking him completely. Goran moaned and moaned and then his eyes opened for a moment and then closed again. Her heart drummed in her temples and it felt more excited to her than during lovemaking. I have done it! I have done it, she repeated her excitement with her inner voice that jumped about and endangered her to cry out.

She had two more syringes and to be used the next days as directed. She checked his pulse. It was up. She covered him with the linen and the lightweight down cover and moved from her position, got up and walked to the lounge cupboard, where Susan kept her liqueur. She poured herself a stiff scotch and signaled Caltis as agreed and he confirmed. Feeling drowsy from the drink, she went to the bathroom, and cleaned herself in the bidet thinking about their lovemaking. She had enjoyed Goran she mused, went back to bed and floated into sleep.

Chapter Thirty
Goran

Susanna wakes and hurries to shower. Goran is in deep sleep and she has a phone call from the clinic. It is urgent for a patient to be treated. She asks for the head nurse. "What is it about?" "Change of bandages and extension of prescribed medicines."

"All right I will be there in ten minutes, meanwhile you can handle it."

"Yes, I will Susan." Susanna dresses in a hurry and as Goran still sleeps she would come back later and check him out for another injection, but this first one holds out pretty well. Chronis calls her and he would come by later, as an outpatient, as agreed. Susanna is on her way and she has not noticed that Goran had stirred. Her head is filled with the clinic procedures and keeping up Susan's image. She parks her car and enters J&S Clinic.

Greg has a strange feeling about recent developments and he contacts his man observing the clinic. "Susan has just arrived."

"Keep on tracking the clinic procedures and her." The man confirms. Greg has driven around following Castor, hoping he will lead him to Caltis who has disappeared. He stops at the shopping mall, where Chronis buys supplies. Greg is waiting in the car ready to pursue him. He has a feeling that these manoeuvres are all a decoy and Caltis has established himself an underground network, dealing habit forming drugs from shipments to and from Piraeus harbour. His man there had reported activities, but he could not get close enough to check the contents in the boxes.

Goran wakes and his vision is blurred. His mobile has been still, but as he falls out of bed and clambers around, he has a problem to activate it. He is thirsty, and he crawls on all fours to the bathroom. He pulls himself up on the rails and drinks cold water, which revives him slowly. Then he showers and enjoys the steam room for a while. Thoughts about yesterday return and he recalls Susan, pleasant, smiling, yet taciturn, but he suspects a foul act on him after their lovemaking. No, Susan would never do that. He racks his brains about any unusual thing, movement, or word that does not fit to Susan, but he cannot come up with anything. Why would Susan inject him with a tranquilizer? He moves to the kitchen and takes the carton of milk, downing it. AH, he sighs, this feels better already. He must contact Greg immediately. Let him check it out. His mobile phone's battery is empty. "Damned," he must have been out for a whole day and night. He fetches the charger from the drawer and then started recharging his mobile, Greg's and Susan's messages appeared in sequence. He read Greg's last message from this morning; "Where are you Goran? Please answer urgently! He pressed the reply button and Greg instantly responds.
"Where are you?"

"I am at Susan's house."

"I am trying to contact you since two days."

"Sorry I was out."

"What do you mean?"

"Knocked out by tranquilizers."

"Stay where you are."

"No I am leaving, find me along the way."

"OK" Greg felt a stab in his stomach. It definitely sounded not like Goran. Something had happened. He pushed his foot down on the accelerator and raced toward Susan's house.

Goran pocketed his gun, donned his jeans and jacket and rushed out the door, heading into the direction of the clinic. He felt damned tired, exhausted and irritated, but spirited. Slowly his mental capacities came alive and his mind tried feverishly to connect up the images that zipped around in front of his eyes. Susan, who appeared younger and slimmer? Showers but not together, like usual, lovemaking different, but not bad for a change. Then he felt the distant prick of a needle. He was out like a falling stone. This is it- he shouted - it's NOT Susan. She would have commented on his Nasi Goreng, her speciality. He had forgotten the raisins. Susan would have detected that immediately. So who was THIS Susan? His knees caved in and he fell at the wayside onto a grassy mound next to the country road.

Greg wondered about Goran and as he contacted his man at the clinic, he reported that a young man had entered. He came out half an hour later and rushed off. Then another car arrived and Susan stepped into the Land Rover and the man drove off with her. After an hour he came back again and she went into the clinic again.

As he instructed his man to stay on, he entered the road to Susan's house. He saw a man collapsing. Greg stopped his car and saw Goran lying at his side.

"Come on Goran, get into the car." He supported him and helped him into the seat, closed the door and rushed off with him. At Greg's safe house, not far from the shopping mall, established after Takis had been taken from their original house, he asked his medical doctor to check Goran out.

"He has dehydration and a poisoning," the doctor said. He put Goran on a vitamin and energy boosting intravenous drip. Goran relaxed and recovered fast. Greg found him up and completely recovered, but filled with anger. "I need to get to the bottom of this Greg. Let's go!"

"Slowly soldier, firstly let's consult intelligence." He used his communication gizmo and informed himself about the status.

"We have entered Chronis' home and secured some video tapes." It's all about Susan." Greg shakes his head. "However, as soon as we had left, he came with another man, probably Castor, Caltis' right hand man. He had an argument with him and it was about the videos, we overheard. Chronis tried to strangle him, but we intervened and captured Chronis, while we let Castor go to lead us to Caltis."

"Well done guys! " Greg's men brought Chronis in and locked him into the interrogation room. The man, who brought the video tapes, set the first tape up on the machine. Greg and Goran studied the tapes.

"Susan's apartment had been bugged." It must have been before Greg had moved in, as Susan appeared alone.

"But why would they video tape Susan?" Goran said.

"One reason only," Greg mused "to study her character."

"I'll be damned!" Goran gasped.

"See on the second tape they had videotaped her in the clinic." Goran shouted.

"Yes, now I get it."

"Let's go and interrogate Chronis." Greg said, stood up and Goran followed.

Chronis had been talking to Susanna at the clinic, to throw in the towel and come with him to the Island of Samos, where he had a hideout at a relative's place.

"How do you think we can get away with Caltis watching us?"

"If we go now we can make it, he urged her on." Susanna thought about the money.

"But I will still get the remainder of my cash."

"He will kill you!" Her eyes turned cold. There was no way he could convince her of the cold and beastly character of Caltis. "Well, take this and keep it in your bag. Careful, it's loaded." He handed her a gun. Susanna took it and placed it in her handbag. Chronis got up, left her office and headed out of the clinic to the parking area. His mobile rang. "Chronis?" It was Castor.

"Yes. What's up?"

"I need the video tapes for Caltis."

"I am on my way home now..."

"OK, see you later." Castor hung up. What the hell does he need the tapes for? Chronis mused. It must have something to do with Susanna. She obviously had fulfilled her usefulness. If she had to disappear, so he had too. It's time he left and he felt sorry for Susanna, but she was a material girl. So be it, he concluded his thoughts and entered his home. He looked for the video tapes, but he could not find them. He was sure he had left them next to the video machine. "Damned!" Somebody must have taken them, but who had been here? Castor parked his car in the driveway and walked to the entrance door.

"Have you got the tapes?"

"I can't find them."

"What does that mean?"

"It means what I say." Chronis became angry.

"Well, I have to kill you if you are lying," Castor said, jumped him and placed a nylon noose around his neck. Surprised by Castor's action Chronis struggled to pull his gun. He felt the thin thread cutting into his throat. As he thought he would expire and say goodbye to this world, he heard a thump and Castor went down. Somebody pulled his arms, strapped him and while he coughed he was placed into the seat of a car and driven off in a hurry. The men dressed in dark gear, looking like security men, kept quiet. One man handed him a lozenge and he recovered from his injured esophagus. His eyes were blindfolded and when the car stopped he was brought into a room that smelled of old potatoes. His blindfold removed, the shutters drawn on the windows, he could not recognize much in the dim lit room. Two men sat at a table. They asked him to sit down.

"Your name?" Chronis knew he faced the opposition of Caltis and he would not hold back answering their questions. After all it was about his survival.

"Chronis."

"Who are you with?"

"Caltis."

"His aide?"

"I used to be."

"And now?"

"I dislike his methods, but I am responsible for Susanna."

"What about the tapes?" Aha Chronis thought they do not know yet.

"Those are for training Susanna."

"Who is that?"

The woman at the clinic."

"Damned!" Goran jumped up, as he connected immediately. "And where is the real Susan?"

Caltis kidnapped her."

"Where is she?" Goran shouted and pulled Chronis' hair snapping his head back. Greg intercepted. "Easy soldier." He turned to Chronis. "Tell us the location."

Chronis swallowed. "Listen I need to have a ticket and a ride to my hideout. If I talk they will kill me. "

"OK, Greg said, "we'll do that."

"Where is she?" Goran bellowed.

"She is at Caltis' safe house." Chronis described the old windmill and the road to it.

"Can I phone Susanna at the clinic?" Goran became alarmed.

"What for?"

"I want to save her from being slaughtered."

"We'll see what we can do," Goran said and asked Greg to come outside.

"We must take action now." Greg agreed but it had to be a military operation. Goran agreed. "But Caltis I take on myself."

"Sure," Greg said and patted his shoulder. "Let's go and do damage."

Chapter Thirty One
Castor

Castor regained consciousness and he informed Caltis that the video tapes had disappeared together with Chronis. "Get the son-of-a-bitch," he shouts.

"I was knocked out when I tried to get Chronis talking."

"Damned, its Goran's security friends," Caltis puffed. "Get me Susanna from the clinic, "he bellowed, "address her as Susan and better make it snappy." Castor hurried to his car and drove to the J&S clinic. He would have to be bold, but just ask her first to come quietly, he thought, thinking about beautiful Susan who was strapped to a chair and at the mercy of the peasant Caltis. He had to make sure he was not rude to her. Security at the clinic let her through as he checked with Susan telling her he had a message from one of her outpatients. When he mentioned Caltis, Susan asked the security officer to let him through.

"Hi Susan," he said, as he entered her office. "Please come with me quietly, as Caltis asked to see you."

"Can't that wait?"

"Believe me he said immediately!" Susanna - sorry Susan." She indeed looks like the other Susan, he thought.

The head nurse passing had turned her head as she overheard Castor's faux pas and wondered what was going on lately with her boss. She definitely had neglected her schedule and she was about to contact Dr Joachim, who was in Germany to complain about the mess. Susanna got up, took her bag and donned her jacket. Castor walked behind her, his fingers on the gun in his pocket pointed at her. He drove and Susanna asked him questions, which he avoided to answer. She became angry and demanded answers, but Castor had his one hand on the wheel and the other one clasping a gun.

Susanna knew she had to be cunning with Caltis in order to stay alive. She resorted to exercise possible answers to have ready for her pending interrogation. She clutched her bag with the loaded gun inside.

Greg's men are concentrated on following Castor, who had driven to the J&S clinic to fetch Susanna. They follow them in the grey Nissan 4x4 that will lead them to Caltis' safe house and probably where Susan is held. "Be careful and stay at a safe distance." Greg had instructed them. In the distance they saw Castor taking the right lane toward the hill, on which a windmill was situated. They stopped their car, hiding it behind cops of acacia trees. One of the men stayed behind in the car. The other man circled the hill, but it was too risky to get close. He signaled Greg that he had to wait for nightfall, as there were no shrubs to approach the safe house without being detected. "Indeed," Greg signaled back, "he probably has a telescope."
"So I'll take the back approach where the ravine is located, below the hill that lead up to the old windmill." Greg confirmed, "Communicate us the state inside if you manage a peek."

Greg's man made his way up at dusk and he could come close to the windmill, but awaited nightfall. As he moved to the back of the safe house, a car arrived. He ducked and saw Castor pushing Susanna ahead of him. They entered the windmill. He had to have an opportunity to look inside, but all windows had been curtained off. He discovered outside access irons fixed into the wall of the tower structure, which lead up to the gear of the jib skeleton and he climbed them. At the first floor window he heard voices and he could see the feet of three men. At the second floor he overheard one voice and it sounded Greek. He communicated his findings to Greg. As he came to the third floor he heard a woman moaning. He listened at the window, where the frame had been damaged and he could hear a man addressing a woman.

"Do you wish to live?" The woman moaned.

"I will cut your tongue off if you do not talk and sign this document!" He heard slaps and beatings and then heavy steps as the man moved down the wooden staircase.

As Greg's scout moved down again, he could hear screaming. It must be the woman they had just brought in. Two different male voices shouted and then he heard "Take her, take her" and a woman screaming. He descended quickly and made his way down to cross from the windmill to the ravine. The entrance door opened and two men appeared. The scout had to duck.

"You gave her a good hiding," the one said in his native language, but the scout could understand basic Greek.

"Damned!" The other said, unbuttoning his fly for a pee. The other joined him.

"You did well Castor," he laughed, "fucking her like a duck." He roared with laughter.

"Well, she had me by the balls, doing what you asked her for. I could not resist."

"That's my boy. Tomorrow I will deal with the other one;" he guffawed and closed his fly.

"Oh the princess? Please don't hurt her."

"Oh that's what you call her?" They laughed and entered the mill again.

Caltis continued Castor's interrogation of Susanna. She had slumped to the floor, feeling kicked about, mistreated by the gangsters and violated by Castor, but at least it was not the brute Caltis. She hoped they would let her go, when she agreed even hesitantly to their demands. Caltis had not believed her that she did not knew where Chronis had put the tapes and about his present whereabouts. The only information Caltis received is that Goran's security guards had taken Chronis hostage. She had been delivered to the knife's edge and she wondered who would toss it into her or cut her into half. There was no doubt about the Brutes, who would stop from nothing to kill her. Susanna was clutching to straws. They had promised her big payments and all she's got were humiliation and rape. She thought hard about how to approach her captors, but could not come up with any ideas. Her mind was empty, Goran had escaped, she had failed to tranquilize him properly, but she blamed it on the syringes they had given her. Damned! She had to play on the other woman-Susan-who they held here too, probably upstairs.

Castor appeared and she started to sweet talk to him.

"Listen my fiery lover, can't you loosen my ties a bit? "

"No way," he said and eyed her body. He enjoyed looking at her.

"Just a bit," Susanna pleaded.

"Caltis will kill me."

"He will kill us all anyway, or what do you think?"

"Well, if you promise me to let me again..." She smiled. She knew she had a sexual edge on him.

"Yes of course, I will show you things you don't even know." She licked her lips. He felt stirred gazing at her insinuations.

"OK, I will come at night."

"Don't take too long." Castor was confused, his mind going nuts for her. He dreamed of her full lips and her shapely derriere.

"No I won't. I will come when all are asleep."

Susanna leaned back and relaxed. She thought about the money she could get to through her potential lover, who desired her. She'd play him and make him so weak that his body would melt between her swollen lips.

Greg awaited the scouts and as soon as they had arrived, he called for a meeting. With Goran again in fighting condition and keen to free Susan and get his hands on Caltis, the meeting was short and to the point.

"Everybody in full battle gear tomorrow at four am. A-group to create a diversion by getting the fighters from the safe house "

"How will we do that?"

"Fighters will rush to the safe house. A messenger will precede them with a message to Caltis." The group looked at each other, querying who it would be.

Greg continued. "We have reliable information from Goran's source that the majority of his group will be surprised early morning, offloading a ship in Piraeus harbour. A man from their camp has been secured and he will rush to the safe house to inform Caltis of the raid. He carries no mobile phone and he does not know Caltis' telephone number. If we can lure a few guys out, we may have a complex battle, as Caltis will rush to his car and order a counter attack.

"Where we do we tackle him?"

"Right at the base of the hill, where the cops of trees are and a brook runs along."

Goran will concentrate on him, while we have to take out his gang."

"How will we free Susan?" Goran asked.

"Well, he might turn back and rush to the safe house, with you in pursuit. You have to get him and free Susan. Can you do it?"

"Of course I can do it, I will make him suffer for everything he caused me, caused you and caused to my friends."

"Hear, hear," Greg's men murmured approval.

"We have to look out for each other though," Greg said. "It's late, let's catch some rest before the cock crows." Greg finished the meeting.

Goran was lost in thought. He reclined on a bunk bed and thought about Susan. She was probably tied up and handled roughly. Caltis obviously tries a last ditched effort to squeeze from her a written agreement to sell her and Cathy's shares of the club. Even if he was sacked he would attempt to have ownership of a company he had stolen from the Goran family. On intuition he phoned his Dad.

"It's time Dad, he informed him." The wording they had agreed to ask Don for backup. "I will be on my toes," Walt replied. Goran smiled and transferred the coordinates of the safe house to his Dad.

Chapter Thirty Two
Goran & Caltis

Goran woke from a dream. Susan had been hung and as he interfered with Caltis, he kicked the supporting chair and Susan would have been strangled, but he kicked the chair back and landed a fatal blow on Caltis, who spun and fell. He rushed with Susan down the stairs, ignoring the hung skeleton of Susanna next to her. Then a rocket hit the windmill and the tower exploded into smithereens...

"Ah! He sighed and was wide awake. The day of battle had arrived finally and he exercised his Tai Chi movements to make his muscles supple and flexible for what he sensed would be a fight for life and death. He dressed carefully into the dark grey battle suit Greg had supplied him with, together with a serrated hunting knife, guns with holsters, a knapsack with ammunition and survival gear, torch and a flare gun.

All ready at four am sharp, the fighters moved with three 4x4's into position at the base of the hill, below the old tower mill. Goran was impatient and hardly could restrain his temper. He decided to meditate.

Greg was positioned further back, ready to attack Caltis' gang when they returned from Piraeus. As soon as Greg received a signal from his scout that the gang was on their way, he alerted his man for the ambush.

Caltis, could not sleep, he paced around in circles at the first floor of his safe house. The floor creaked and it woke Susanna. She had been seeing Castor, who was nuts about making love to her and she had tamed him the way she wanted. He melted in her oral attentions. He had to promise Susanna to free her and show him the cashbox, as she was owed money from Caltis for her services at the clinic and as a false Susan for the time the real Susan had been kidnapped. But now Caltis had broken his promise to pay her and Susan was still a prisoner upstairs. He intended to molest her this morning. She could hear her cries, muffled through a tape they must have stuck across her mouth. What Brutes, she thought and made eyes at Caltis, who came downstairs having been phoned. It must have been urgent, as he stopped at her and shouted "Do you wish to redeem yourself and get the money?"

"Yes, she answered," surprised. "What must I do?"

"KILL HER!" He pointed upstairs. He handed her a knife. Susanna took her bag along, where she had the gun from Chronis. Then she made her way upstairs. Caltis rushed out the door, his staff swarming all over the place. He commanded them to their battle positions and shouted "Downhill, downhill, they have attacked us!"

Greg's man had ambushed Caltis' gang who came in two Range Rovers past the engagement point. A fight ensued and as the men jumped from the vehicles, it became a man to man fight. Greg's men seemed to have the upper hand and Goran had a good day, supporting him with his fighting style. He brought down a few men and looked out for Caltis. The driver of one Range Rover sped off, but a sharpshooter of Greg's group finished him. He lost control and the car rolled over, bursting into flames. In the smoke and battle heat Greg had not noticed Caltis' back-up gang and his men were attacked. The battle was fierce and Greg called for spreading out to take cover. There was a huge explosion as a rocket hit the vehicle of the back-up gang and bodies were flung through the air with gnarled and bent metal parts. It smelled of cordite and burning rubber.

Caltis had summoned his men from the safe house and left in a hurry, rushing downhill with guns firing until a grenade brought some of his men down. He noticed men with balaclavas in black gear who did not belong to Goran's men, but supported him. When all his men were shot, he jumped the gun and raced back uphill. Goran had a lookout for him and he could not engage him, as Don's soldiers took care of Caltis' men. Goran signaled them and rushed behind the fleeing Caltis. At the top of the hill he cornered him and pointed his gun at him. "It's over Caltis, surrender."
"Not after a man to man fight."
"Where is Susan?"
"You will find out soon." Caltis took a stance.
"Tai Chi to death!" Goran shouted and pushing hands landed a blow to Caltis ribs. Caltis collapsed but recovered and he retaliated, but Goran felt he had the edge, delivering blow after blow. Caltis took an opportunity and stormed into the windmill. Goran cornered him at the stair and delivered him a blow that set him reel-

ing. The tough training with Greg had made him into a kick-boxing fast fighter and Caltis felt he was at his wits and physical end. Calling Susanna, he created a deviation, pulled his knife and attacked Goran, who was cut on his arm, but could counter the blow and wrestle his arm twisting it hard. It hurt Caltis and Goran kicked it dislocating it from his shoulder. Caltis cried out, fell on the deck, his knife slid to the corner. He clutched his arm. Goran stormed upstairs to find Susan. He was shocked. Susan had a rope around her neck slung from the roof beam above. She stood on a chair which this other Susan intended to kick aside, wielding a knife in her hand.

"You devil and false Susan," he shouted and kicked boxed false Susan aside, who dropped the knife and collapsed. Goran stabilized Susan on the chair stepped up on the ladder behind her and cut the rope. It smelled of decay. He noticed a skeleton next to her.

"The hanging beam," he said and kissed Susan. "Oh Goran…what took you so long? She sighed. "Watch out!" Caltis was coming up the stairs with a gun in his left hand.

"I have you cornered you turtle doves," he grinned." Say your prayers. A shot rang out and Caltis had a strange look on his face, when he collapsed broke through the hand railing and fell down to the second ground floor. Susan looked at her namesake the false Susan who held a gun in her hand.

"Give me the gun, Susanna," Goran said and she pleaded to find her money first.

"I make sure that you get your money," Goran said and took the gun off her. Susanna ran downstairs, opened Caltis' sea trunk and retrieved her money. Then she fled. Goran took Susan downstairs. He noticed how weak she was on her feet. As they arrived at the ground floor his cellphone rang.

"Yes, Goran."

"Do you have Susan?"

"Yes, she is OK."

"Get out there. Don's men want to blow it up."

"Wait there is ammunition and a cashbox here, tell them!"

"OK"

Two men with balaclavas on their heads entered and greeted him. Goran pointed to the sea trunk. They took the box out and searched for weapons.

"Under the floor boards, Susan said."

Goran supported Susan and called for Greg's 4x4. But Greg did not answer. He supported Susan to walk to Caltis' 4x4, mounted his kerchief on the antenna and drove her downhill. Greg's men were at the base and they took possession of the vehicle and helped Susan into their medical van where the doctor looked after her.

"We better take her to the clinic. It's safer for her there." Goran directed the driver. The moment they turned the narrow road away from the hill, they heard a huge explosion. Don's men had blown up Caltis' safe place. The shards rained down towards Greg's vehicles and his men, who collected all weapons and gear from Caltis' dead gang members. They had agreed with the balaclava men that they would leave the bodies for them to ferry away. The dark clothed men cleaned up with speed, professionally loaded all onto an army truck and disappeared with their van ahead.

"Where is Greg?" Goran asked the driver.

"He's at the clinic."

"How is he?"

"Wounded but he will survive."

"Thanks god," Goran sighed. It would have been a great pain to lose the great strategist and saviour of Susan and himself. Goran's mobile phone beeped.

"You had a good day?" It was his Dad.

"Yes, the eagle has landed." His Dad chuckled.

"I did expect nothing else."

Arriving in the safe surrounds of Susan's clinic, Dr Joachim and staff welcomed Susan. She was ushered into the examination room, where Dr Joachim had a look at her. Greg's doctor had administered a drip for nourishment. "She was badly dehydrated and in shock," he said and Dr Joachim lauded his expertise. "I have been in many situations like these," he said and Dr Joachim nodded.

"I can see that. Thanks for your help."

The staff had prepared welcome drinks and sandwiches and a happy mood spread out fast, with stories about false Susan and her inability to act decisively, leaving decisions to the head nurse, until Dr Joachim rushed back, as she had phoned him in Munich.

Goran visited Greg, who was in intensive care, having collected two bullets.

"Damned!" he said the bullet proof vest was hit but two bullets hit me just at the edge. Thanks to the medical staff I was saved from bleeding to death."

"I am glad you are all right Goran."

"Nice to seeing you Greg." They talked about the battle with Caltis' gang.

"Our strategy nearly backfired on us, as we forgot about Caltis' back-up gang."

"Well, there were the balaclava helpers for us."

"Tell me, were they Don's men?"

"We had an agreement, Dad's brokerage."

"Greetings and thanks to your Dad," Greg said and lied down again.

"I will check on you later, now have a rest." He left the room and joined the party. The head nurse handed him a drink.

"Let me look at your arm." Goran still had his blood stained shirt on where Caltis had wounded him with a knife.

"This will need attention." She asked her nurse to apply bandages.

Goran made his way to see Susan. She was sitting in bed and checking her mobile phone the head nurse had brought to her.

"You should rest and not work Susan."

"Hi Goran, I have not realized how much work had been piled up on my clinical plate." She smiled. "They have taken care of your injury."

"I am glad you are well soon." He bent down and kissed her.

"Mh Goran you taste good, even with the battle smell still around your gear."

"I will go and shower, but first let me toast to you."

"Cheers, Susan said, I get mine intravenously." She laughed. He had missed her laugh and it told him that she was well on her way to recovery. He drained his glass with a few gulps. It was the best scotch he had ever had.

Chapter Thirty Three
Susan & Goran

Susan had recovered and she woke in the bed of her clinic. The first thing she saw was Goran's face. He kissed her. "I will take care of you," he said and she got out of her bed. Goran accompanied her to the bathroom. He tested the water while she took her hospital robe off. Let me pamper you. He doffed his garb, entered the generous shower cubicle and soaped her body. Susan felt as good as she had never felt before in her life, letting herself go, handing herself over to her lover and saviour, melting to a lightness that she had not experienced before, perhaps at one point with Kathy, but when it had been in the presence of Goran. Then she had never thought that she would also receive other shades of love from the skilled and hard fighter: compassion, dedication and caring. His touches became sensational on her skin and when he kissed her she stirred and a flash of passion for him rose from the pit of her belly.

Goran experienced love which went far beyond the pure passionate embraces and losing himself in the throes of lust Susan could evoke in him. He recalled Kathy and the pleasure the three of them had together. Yet through this love he had changed into the man he saw for himself: as hard as he became in fighting for justice and for honours in Tai Chi engagements, as gentle and soft he had become towards Susan, who responded to him as if he still would love two women. Kathy's spirit had slipped into Susan's and this phenomenon had taken complete possession of his being. He soaped Susan's body and enjoyed stroking its shapely undulations, caressing its folds and sculpted landscapes. Her stretching reactions turned him on and he embraced her slippery body with kisses under the spray of warm water his senses became alive, his being transformed into light feathers, he experienced a metamorphosis with Susan placing her legs around his waist as he lifted her up and their heated movements became a physical passion, which their souls left behind soaring in an incredible lightness, two white birds towards the blue sky.

"Oh Goran, love!" Susan sighed and still held on to her love as if she would be afraid to fall from the lofty heights she had felt flying up to.

"My precious Susan." Goran whispered still breathing faster. These moments of sensual lovemaking had been unusual and special to him and he sensed to her as well. He sat down on the bench and Susan straddled his lap and they sat for some time, forgetting time and matter, completely moving as one person combined, one body and one soul, or was it that they had flown off to another world in which there was only love and no hate and not one single thought about a material world.

"Goran," Susan whispered into his ear, "my tantric lover." He smiled, as he became aware of Susan's feelings the same way as she became aware of his. The ongoing intensity of it made them feel as an embrace of their souls and they forgot about time.

Greg had been healed and he already walked about on his daily routine along the passages of the clinic. Susan had instructed her head nurse to take good care of the burly worrier, who had been more than just a hired hand for their security. He gave them much more than fighting the gang of Caltis, he gave them his friendship. He stopped at Susan's office and noticed she was not here yet.

"Good morning Greg," the head nurse appeared. "I see you are fit and healthy."

"Thank you, I feel much better, about 70 percent." He smiled.

"Looking for Susan?"

"Yes, I wanted to say hello."

"She will be in soon."

"Is she all right?"

"I think she has experienced a rebirth." The head nurse smiled and excused herself. Greg thought of Goran and her having a good time. As he walked about and became more and more impressed by the excellent facility Susan had created with her partner Dr Joachim, he mused about his future. His wounds had healed but he was getting on with age and his fighting times as a mercenary came to an end. He came to the entrance hall and checked on the security offices. He greeted the officer on duty and his eyes scanned the security installation. It is still in working order, but technology had moved on and a well-designed update was needed. He would mention this to Susan, whenever he had an opportunity to speak to her. The safe house of his men will become abandoned soon, as all has to be cleared out and the equipment had to be stored. He would have a meeting with his right hand man, Bill, and they had to take a decision what to do further. Greg had some ideas up his sleeve he would work around in his mind until a viable solution presented itself. He had released Chronis, who took Susanna and left for the island of Samos.

With Caltis and his gang eradicated, Goran had taken on new responsibilities and started to rebuild the local MAC, which had been run down by Caltis and he had plans of extensions. An important meeting had been scheduled with an architect, who had been chosen by Walt the acting president, to present a scheme for the extensions as discussed at a previous meeting. Goran looked forward to it. He felt a new energy that his daily exercises of Tai Chi were not only unlocking, but pushing forward like a fount that had turned from a brook into a stream of ideas and a never tiring approach to his new life with Susan. She meant everything to him. Besides of her medical abilities, she had become a model of caring and compassion, a sensual woman of golden appearance and a heart for the disadvantaged. But she embodied all he had ever wished for in life, two beings, Kathy and Susan, Kathy's artistic and intuitive spirit and Susan's crystalline structures of intellect.

The party for accepting the new scheme for the MAC at Susan's house had been in full swing. While Greg and his men, who stayed with him behind, organized security, Susan greeted her guests with Goran at her side. The music challenged the guests for a dance and the laid out food on a buffet looked appetizing. Walt clinked his glass with a spoon and asked for attention.

"I don't want to bore you with a long speech. I have a surprise for Goran and Susan, but for all who are members of our MAC's that have done well and as you know, will start expanding with our local main club. I have to tell you that we have to celebrate the forthcoming start of building operations sponsored by a dear friend." Everybody clapped hands and Walt raised his glass. Cheers to a great future."

Suddenly Goran stepped forward and thanked his Dad. He praised Greg and his dedicated men who fought against powerful odds together with him and he remembered the brave journalist who helped him with sourcing Greg, but who had lost his life. He thanked Kathy, who had given her life and he thanked all his friends and Greg and his men who supported him through thick and thin and in the process became his dear friends. He intended to train at MAC with the aim to fight for the upcoming European Masters Championships in Tai Chi. His guests cheered and he raised his arms. "Finally I have an announcement to make: Susan and I are engaged." He kissed her. She smiled and raised her hand asking to say a few words. She felt her new ring on her finger and watched its sparkle for a moment.

"I have been building a successful clinic and would not stand here to in front of you, if it would not have been for the love and help of caring Walt, Greg, who watched over me, Joachim, who steered the clinic when my life was in danger and for Goran, who risked his own life to save mine. I am fortunate to be blessed with loyal friends, to have a family that is filled with love and a man at my side that means more to me than all material possessions. However, I have decided with my partner Dr Joachim to appoint Greg and his security company to look after us and all who will care to join his services."

Greg came forward and thanked her "I am happy for Susan and Goran. I have looked after them professionally and with the best of my ability and that of my dedicated men. We have stood shoulder to shoulder in battle and we poured our hearts out to each other as true friends. I thank them for their trust in me and I am happy to be part of this wonderful family."

The sudden noise of sounds like shots cracked into the silent atmosphere and Greg became alert and moved to the terrace.

Walt exclaimed with a broad smile "Greek fire! Worthy of a great celebration. "Greg relaxed as all laughed and enjoyed the colourful spectacle that rose with a soaring swooshing sound into the skies and burst into a myriad of colourful shooting stars, the stuff of which dreams are made off.

Fin.

About the author.

Born in Eastern Austria, close to the Hungarian border, he witnessed as a young man the horrors of a nation's suppression, erupting in the Hungarian Revolution of 1956. He finished his education in art and architecture in Vienna, married and sailed for the Cape of Africa, an adventure that followed his childhood dreams. He had drawn African animals for his art classes, but the time had come to see them in their natural habitat.

Meeting a varied facet of people and cultures, working as a draughtsman in an engineering office, as an architect for a cultural centre, as a coordinator of craftsmen and professionals, he made good use of his language skills traveling throughout Southern Africa.
During a trip to Lesotho, a native artist showed him rock paintings with their stark palimpsest outlines and with typified movements of animals and humans. It made a lasting impression on him and influenced his artistic work.

His vast collection of drawings and slides had been lost during a change of domiciles, but further studies about the art of the San-people reawakened his dormant artistic longing for expression of his art, filling sketch-books with drawings and notepads with poetry and prose.

While revisiting the capitals of Europe, he sensed the bond of art being borderless and free, reaching out across continents into the world.

During a visit to Greece, he was accepted into a circle of artists and poets, who encouraged him continuing his art and a friend introduced him to the works of famous Greek poets.

In South Africa he joined writing and poetry workshops of *Writers Write.* It was to open the floodgates of his creativity.

He decided to travel through Greece and visits its sites of antiquity, read up on Classical mythology and to enjoy translations of Greek poetry and prose.

Settled in 2013/14 in Klosterneuburg-Weidling, a historic and romantic village, part of the culturally important city of Klosterneuburg, where he now lives and prepares his poetry and novels for publication. In painting his poetry, he has established his series of paintings and drawings, he calls *Mystical Realism*. Poet Nikolaus Lenau is buried here, and Franz Kafka had visited. Their writings will be always an inspiration.

Further books by the author at the BoD-bookshop:

KING OF ICE. A poetic lore
SPLEEN OF LOVE. Zen and the Lake Moeris adventure.
THE FABRICATOR. Life and Death of a great canvas.